DARK GLASS

A Montague and Strong Detective Agency Novel

ORLANDO A. SANCHEZ

This is a work of fiction. All of the characters, organizations, and events portrayed in this novel are either products of the authors' imagination or are used fictitiously and are not to be construed as real. Any resemblance to actual events, locales, organizations, or persons, living or dead, is entirely coincidental.

© 2020 Orlando A. Sanchez

All rights reserved, including the right to reproduce this book, or portions thereof, in any form.

Published by: Bitten Peaches Publishing

Cover Art: Deranged Doctor Design www.derangeddoctordesign.com

DESCRIPTION

Sometimes, being immortal can get you killed.

When Fate pays Simon a visit accusing him of disrupting causality, she makes him an offer he can't refuse—become mortal or die.

There's only one small problem.

In order to become mortal, Simon must find the goddess, Kali the Destroyer, and convince her to remove her curse. To complicate matters further, Haven and Roxanne are under attack by an ancient spell-an entropic sphere designed to kill everyone inside the facility.

Now, Monty and Simon must find out why Simon is disrupting causality, stop a lethal sphere from killing innocents, and convince an angry goddess to lift a curse.

A typical day in the Montague and Strong Detective Agency.

Join the Trio of Terror as they discover that not everything is as it seems, and sometimes, the past can kill you.

"For now we see through a glass, darkly; but then face to face: now I know in part; but then shall I know even as also I am known."

1Corinthians 13:12

ONE

I woke up to a delicate tongue-slapping.

"What...what?" I said, pushing my hellhound away from my face. "I don't need a tongue bath. What is it?"

<You were sleeping.>

<Yes, I was. Now I'm awake. What's with the tongue-lashing?

>

<You were making noise.>

<Noise? What noise? I don't make noises in my sleep.>

<Did you eat some bad meat? The noise sounded like you hurt your stomach.>

<I didn't eat bad meat and my stomach is fine. I'm fine.>

<I know. I licked you. Now you will be better. Stop eating bad meat.>

He padded off and left me alone.

I laid my head back on my pillow and realized how surreal my life had become. For once, there were no angry gods or world-ending cataclysms on the schedule. I had a moment to actually bask in doing...nothing.

I never anticipated being cursed alive by Kali, bonding

to a hellhound, and working cases with a grouchy mage. I couldn't even begin to explain my complicated relationship with an ancient vampire.

Despite my several near-death moments, I wouldn't trade it in for a 'normal life'. It was clear my brain was still tired. I had the perfect solution. Deathwish with a splash of javambrosia would right all wrongs this morning.

I jumped out of bed, and nearly faceplanted as I crashed into the immobile object known as Peaches. He had the bad habit of materializing in the oddest places and at the strangest times.

"What did I tell you about doing that?" I said, catching my balance before introducing my face to the floor. "Walk around the house...*walk*. Not 'blink in-between and give me a heart attack'."

<You said to stay out of the bathroom when you make it smell bad. This is your sleeping room.>

<Yes, don't blink around my bedroom either. Not before I've had coffee.>

<This room smells too.>

<You realize it smells mostly of overfed hellhound, right?>

<Is this where you keep the bad meat?>

<What are you talking about?>

He sniffed the air around the bed and chuffed.

<Are you still sick? I can lick you again.>

Now I was getting concerned. It was one thing for him to accuse me of making noises when I slept (which, for the record, I didn't), it was something else entirely when he started smelling things as off.

<Where does it smell? The room or me?>

He stepped close, sniffed me, and shook his head, slobbering my face.

<You smell different. Did you eat more bad meat?>

I wiped the slobber from my face.

<I didn't eat bad meat. Let's go ask Monty.>

<I'm hungry. Can you fill my bowl?>

<You just ate last night. Maybe you should give your bottomless pit of a stomach a break? I hear fasting is good for you.>

<Fasting? Is that when I eat meat and you tell me to slow down?>

<No. Fasting is when you don't eat for a period of time, to let your stomach rest.>

<It's a curse then?>

<What? No. Fasting is good for you.>

<Eating is good for me. My stomach doesn't need rest. It's not tired.>

<I've noticed. Where's Monty?>

<The angry man is in the room with the big table.>

The room with the 'big table' was our conference room. I got dressed, washed my face of Peaches' magical slobber, and headed to the kitchen. A kettle was whistling on the stove as Monty came in, holding a book.

"Peaches says I smell," I said, pouring my Deathwish Extreme. "What do you think that means?"

"Perhaps it's time for a shower?" Monty said, glancing down at my hellhound. "Animals have a keen sense for these sorts of things."

"Morning English humor," I said. "My day can't get off to a better start. I'm serious. He says I smell different."

"Different how?" Monty now asked, concerned. "Can he clarify?"

"Like I ate bad meat."

"Did you?"

"You two are on a roll today," I said. "I don't eat bad meat."

"Just eliminating the possibilities," he said, putting a teabag into the water. "Your diet is questionable at times."

"Just because I prefer to eat meat over leaves, doesn't mean I eat poorly."

<Meat is life.>

"Exactly. Meat is life," I said, looking down at Peaches who held his titanium bowl in his jaws. "The Zen Meat Master has spoken."

Peaches dropped his bowl with a thud, nearly crushing my toes in the process.

<I'm hungry. I haven't eaten in so long. Are you trying to fast my stomach?>

<Hold on, you black hole. I'm trying to tell Monty what you said.>

<Meat is life?>

<No—I mean yes, meat is life—but I'm talking about the other thing. About my smell.>

<It's not you. It's the air around you.>

"He says it's not me," I repeated, feeling like any moment now I'd be sharing about little Timmy who fell down a well and needed rescuing. "It's the air around me."

"The air around you? Do you have gas?"

I stared at Monty.

"Seriously?"

"I keep telling you those late night snacks will be the death of you," he said, wagging a finger. "It appears your creature agrees. You could stand to eat a salad every now and then."

"Let's forget about my eating habits for a moment and

pretend this is serious," I said. "Can you do your squinty Eastwood thing on my energy signature?"

"I do not do a 'squinty Eastwood thing', I shift spectrums by focusing my vision," Monty said. "This allows me to see irregularities in energy signatures. All mages can do this."

"Right," I answered. "Your squinty Eastwood glare... can you do that?"

"If you insist," Monty said, pouring the boiling water onto the tea leaves. "I still think a good salad will set you right."

"Indulge me."

Monty put the kettle down, narrowed his eyes, and looked at me. His expression grew serious, I mean it became more serious than his resting scowl face.

"What is it?" I asked, concerned. "Your face looks extra scowly."

"Your energy signature."

"What about it? What's wrong?"

"It's phasing, expanding and contracting," Monty answered. "I've never seen anything like it in a non-mage. How did I not sense this?"

"That sounds bad. It's not supposed to do that, is it?"

"We all vibrate at a specific frequency, everything does—"

"Can I have the non-Ziller explanation?" I asked. "I haven't had my coffee yet. My brain is fragile right now."

"Phasing only happens to mages when they shift," he said. "Since you aren't a mage, I have no concrete explanation for what is happening to you. Your frequency is fluctuating, which usually means you are dying, and leaving this plane of existence."

“I don’t do the dying thing though,” I said, confused. “Kali made sure of that.”

“I know,” Monty answered. “That only leaves one other possibility.”

“Why do I get the feeling I’m not going to be thrilled to hear this other possibility?”

“It could be that your specific condition has allowed you to absorb an abundance of runic energy,” Monty said, “causing a catastrophic breakdown of your signature as a side effect.”

“Oh, that’s all?” I said. “Would you mind explaining that in English now?”

“It appears you’re poisoned and dying.”

TWO

I heard the words, but my brain couldn't or wouldn't process them.

"What do you mean, I'm dying? That's impossible. Cursed alive, remember?"

"Well, it seems like you have been exposed to too much energy," Monty began, in his best college lecturer voice. "Think of runic energy as radiation. A small amount is harmless, like sitting on the beach in the summer sun. Too much exposure over a prolonged period and—"

"You get a sunburn," I said, still somewhat confused but getting the gist. "You're saying I've been runically burned?"

"What I'm seeing in your signature would be closer to sun poisoning," Monty answered. "Do you feel any nausea? Are you having any hallucinations or odd thoughts?"

"Only when we teleport."

"What about odd thoughts?"

"Does the fact that you fling energy orbs around, or

that I can mentally speak to my hellhound count as hallucinations or odd thoughts?"

"Neither. I was referring to you having thoughts about casting specific powerful spells, or moments of time dilation or constriction."

"Casting specific spells? I'm not a mage, Monty. As for time being diluted, it feels the same as always, one-hundred percent pure madness."

"Dilation, not dilution," Monty corrected. "Time doesn't feel strange or odd to you?"

"Strange or odd?" I asked. "Why would it? I mean, I have a grumpy mage partner, a hellhound bondmate, and I can, surprisingly, cast some magic. Who knew?"

"What do you mean...grumpy? I was referring to—"

"I also have a weapon inside of me somewhere, we've dealt with gods—one of which cursed me alive—creatures I thought never existed, all kinds of magic and magic-users, some friendly, most deadly."

"Yes, this is all true, what I meant—"

"I've been stabbed, blown up multiple times, crushed, teleported enough times that thinking about it makes my stomach turn, shot, crushed some more, blasted by orbs, subjected to miscellaneous magic, nearly disintegrated with the first Goat, and oh, even killed."

"It would seem that—"

"In addition, I have a 'relationship' with a vampire...a vampire who even *I* don't understand. Complicated doesn't begin to describe it. To top it all off, I get blamed for the destruction caused by mages—present company included—and by other assorted creatures that wreak havoc in our city. So you tell me, Monty, which part qualifies as strange or odd?"

"You seem distressed."

"You just told me I'm poisoned and dying! How did you think I would I react?"

"I think it may be time for a short period of vacation."

"You think?" I scoffed. "Where to? Hades? I hear the underworld is great this time of year."

"That's actually not a bad suggestion," Monty said. "It is out of the way and somewhat secluded. You could even invite your vampire."

"I will," I said, nodding. "If *you* invite Roxanne."

"I'm not the one who needs to destress," he said, quickly. "This vacation is primarily for *your* peace of mind."

"My mind is already in pieces. Haven't you noticed?"

"On more than one occasion, yes. We can discuss the vacation another time."

"Or you just don't want to invite Roxanne to a secluded getaway...in Hades?"

"Your humor, as usual, never ceases to disappoint," he said. "Maybe you should go alone, with your creature? That way we *both* get a vacation."

"I hope to one day be able to match your level of drollery," I mocked. "Can we deal with my catastrophic life-ending energy signature first?"

It was clear I needed my coffee. I took a long pull of Deathwish, reactivating my grumpy brain into some sort of activity.

"Indeed," he said. "Dealing with your current condition takes precedence."

"Sorry," I said and meant it. "I was just looking forward to some downtime from not saving the city, or the Earth, or reality as we know it."

"Downtime? Perhaps when we have a window of relative calm. Possible, but unlikely."

"We are a detective agency," I said. "At no point are those words supposed to include 'for the supernatural community', 'rampant creatures of destruction', or 'solving world-ending cases'."

"And yet here we are," Monty answered matter-of-factly. "It seems you attract these situations."

"I...attract?" I asked. "This all started with Kali and her curse."

"On a case you accepted."

"Not my fault," I said. "You know I had to take that case. There were kids involved."

"I recall," Monty said, " but if you look for a common denominator, a thread that ties it all together...it would be *you*."

It took all of five seconds for my brain to agree. I would need to re-evaluate what I was 'attracting' in my life. In the meantime, I needed to find out what was wrong.

"What do I need to do?" I asked. "About the runic melting, not my attracting chaos."

"Hmm," he said, tapping his chin. "There is one test I can run, but it's usually reserved for mages. I've never tried it on a non-mage."

"Is it dangerous?"

"It's a runic scan of sorts, used to determine power levels, except it's an extra-planar process."

"Extra-planar?" I asked, confused. "Can't we do this at the Golden Circle? Isn't that your mage batcave?"

"I don't have a mage batcave."

"What about with Erik at the Hellfire?"

"This test can't be conducted on our plane. It deals

with a volatile power that would react poorly with the ambient energy. It needs to be extra-planar."

"I don't recall hearing your answer...is it dangerous?"

"Considerably," he said. "Though I don't know how your cursed body will react. It could be fine, or you could be atomized. I wonder if you could return from that kind of trauma?"

"Wonderful," I said. "Now you sound like Hades in his quest to test my immortality. Is there another option?"

"We could let whatever it is run its course. However, I think the end result would be detrimental, but fascinating."

"Don't try so hard to cheer me up, Spock."

"There is much to be said for dispassionate logic in moments like this," Monty answered, with a nod. "It allows for the clinical observation of facts without emotion clouding said observation."

I stared at him.

"There's also much to be said for the passionate losing of your shit when you are informed that overexposure to runic energy may be melting you," I said, raising my voice. "It allows for the repeated pummeling of those who provide said clinical observations."

I took several deep breaths and calmed myself.

"Duly noted," Monty said. "I strongly suggest against trying to pummel me."

"Let's just do this test of yours," I said. "What's a little more pain and danger? I call that breakfast in my world."

"There is one site," Monty said. "Getting there may be a bit tricky, but It should be safer than the alternative."

"Safer? For who?"

"For the general public," Monty answered, still looking

around. “If something goes awry, not that it will, but if it does, it could destroy most of the Moscow. I’d prefer not to revisit that scenario after the deep freeze with Cecelia. Olga would be displeased.”

“Displeased? Olga would crush us...well, *you*.”

“More likely she would freeze us solid first...then crush *us*.”

“Where then?”

“Let’s use my uncle’s room,” Monty said, pointing down the corridor to Dex’s room. “That should suffice.”

“Before we start my torture, can we feed the bottomless pit that is my hellhound?”

Monty looked down at Peaches, who was giving him his best version of puppy dog eyes complete with a grin. With Peaches’ glowing red eyes and ginormous fangs, the effect was just this side of terrifying.

“Is that supposed to be a smile?” Monty asked, still looking at Peaches.

“Yes, it’s a work in progress,” I answered, glancing down at my hellhound. “Nice, huh?”

“It’s about as endearing as a dragon’s snarl,” Monty said. “I’d advise against it.”

Monty gestured, and several large links of sausage appeared before Peaches.

<Good smile, boy. Eat it slow and make sure to say thank you.>

Peaches proceeded to instantly hoover the meat into his never-ending belly. It took all of one second, possibly less.

<I thought you wanted me to eat fast?>

<I said, you should—never mind. Make sure you say thank you.>

Peaches took a small breath and let out a controlled bark that shook the windows.

"He says: 'thank you'," I said, wincing as I slowly shook my head. "That hurt."

"You may want to work on that too," Monty said, rubbing an ear. "A nod would suffice."

"He's still a puppy," I said, rubbing Peaches' massive head. "He's a work in progress."

"Indeed," Monty said as he picked up his cup and headed down the corridor. "I shudder to think about your creature as an adult."

"We'll need a bigger space for him, I think."

"Of course, we'll find something appropriate," Monty said, stopping in front of Dex's door. "Like a football stadium."

I looked at the door. It was covered with faintly glowing, green runes that pulsed to an unknown rhythm. Nothing about this door said 'come in'. The impression it gave off was closer to 'open me and get your ass blasted down the corridor'. I could almost hear Dex's voice, followed by his laugh.

"Why are the runes fading in and out?" I asked. "It's like they're drawing power from something."

"That's different," Monty answered, examining the runes. "I'll have to look into that when I have more time."

"You do realize Dex's room is still *in* The Moscow?" I asked. "This doesn't count as extra-planar."

"Yes and no," Monty answered, examining the runes on the door, and placing his cup on a small table near the door. "The door is somewhat in-between on this plane because of the symbols my uncle used."

"In between this plane and what?" I asked, looking warily at the door. "Those runes look painful."

"Because they are," Monty said, touching several of the symbols in sequence. "If I get the sequence wrong—"

"We get blasted down the corridor?"

"Not exactly," Monty said. "My uncle is a master at teleportation. These runes are designed to prevent anyone from breaking into his space. An incorrect sequence would instantly teleport the offender to some undisclosed locations."

"Locations?" I asked. "You mean it teleports the person to more than one more location, in sequence?"

"Not exactly," Monty said, focusing on the door. "It teleports the person to more than one location instantly—in pieces."

I backed up several feet from the door.

"If you don't mind, I'm going to stand over here."

"Doesn't matter," Monty said with a small shake of the head. "The area of effect on this casting is a particularly nasty piece of work—cunning, devious, and powerful—very much like my uncle. You could, in all likelihood, stand downstairs in the lobby and still be hit by it."

"Why would Dex cast something like that?"

"Because he's my uncle?"

"That actually explains much of it," I answered. "I mean, he is seeing the Morrigan. Dex must have the ultimate deathwish"—I held up my coffee mug—"see what I did there?"

"Really?" Monty said with a small groan. "Maybe you should step back a little farther...like the Randy Rump?"

"Maybe I can help," I said. "I can almost make out some of the runes."

"Only if you want to hasten our demise."

"Let me know if you need assistance," I said backing up farther, "those runes look tricky."

"Thank you. I'm going to need a bit of focus for this part, if you don't mind," Monty said, somewhat distracted as he began the sequence. "I'd hate to visit several dimensions at once. We need to go to a specific location for this test."

Monty began touching some of the symbols, relocating some and rotating others. I wouldn't even know where to begin, much less know what sequence would take us to where we were going.

"Looks complicated."

"Because it is," Monty said without turning. "I've heard silence is instrumental in aiding focus, particularly when dealing with lethal runes."

"Good point," I said, nodding and backing up even more. "Just in case, I'll be over here."

"Mmhmm," Monty answered, still touching symbols in sequence. "This should be the last symbol. We should arrive there at midday."

"Wouldn't it be easier to get around a strange place under the cover of night?"

"That would be logical except this location is extremely dangerous at night."

"Is it dangerous during the day?"

"Yes, but decidedly less lethal than the night."

"Are you sure you got the sequence on those runes right?" I asked, looking at the softly glowing runes. "What happens if you get it wrong?"

"If I'm wrong, we won't be here to discuss it."

"My life is a never-ending adventure," I grumbled. "No

wonder I'm melting inside. It's not runic anything. It's probably just plain mage induced stress."

Monty pressed the last symbol, triggering a bright green, blinding flash. A moment later, the door clicked open.

"Let's go," Monty said. "We want to make sure we maintain the integrity of the space behind this door. Leaving it open for too long is inviting disaster."

"Why?" I asked, reconsidering going into Dex's room. "Where does it lead?"

"You understand the concept of time and relative dimension in space?" Monty asked. "One of the concepts the Moving Market is based on?"

"I understand that sometimes things are bigger on the inside than they appear on the outside."

"Then you know the answer to the question: 'Where does it lead?'"

"No, I don't," I said, frustrated. "That's why I asked. Not that you didn't make it sound incredibly inviting or anything. Where does this door lead?"

He opened the door, and I saw a large green field. It looked like Central Park, but it wasn't the Central Park I was familiar with. I didn't remember the park having a real castle in it. I took one last sip of my Deathwish, realizing how appropriate the name seemed as I looked into the alternate Central Park.

"It leads everywhere."

THREE

"What is this place?" I asked, stepping past the threshold of the door and into the green field. "This looks like Central Park, except I don't remember that building."

"Keep."

"I don't want to," I said, not understanding. "What do you want me to keep?"

"That small fortress"—Monty pointed to the building in the distance—"is referred to as a Keep," he clarified. "Not just 'a building', but a Keep. Specifically the Hunter's Keep, in this case."

"Fine...a Keep," I said. "Why are we headed in that direction?"

"We need to conduct this test inside its walls, and we need to do so before it gets dark. Don't dally," Monty said, walking towards the Hunter's Keep. "I know it looks close, but distance in this place is not always something that can be measured. It's...flexible."

"How can distance be flexible?" I asked. "A meter is a meter."

"Except when it isn't."

"What are you talking about?" I asked. "That 'Keep' can't be more than a kilometer away."

"Yes, and we need to get there immediately," Monty said, his voice laced with urgency. "Let's move."

Peaches unleashed a low growl next to me.

<*What is it boy?*>

<*This place smells bad.*>

<*Can you be clearer?*>

<*Bad smells everywhere.*>

<*Are they close?*>

<*No, but the smell is all around.*>

<*Does it smell the same way I smelled?*>

<*No, it smells like bad dogs.*>

<*Shadowhounds? You smell Shadowhounds?*>

<*Yes, the bad dogs.*>

"According to my trusty hellhound smell detector, we are currently surrounded by nastiness," I said, trying to keep the fear out of my voice. "Shadowhounds, to be precise."

"In this place, they are called Dreadwolves."

"You know about them?"

"Professor Ziller has written an entire treatise on extra-planar creatures," Monty answered. "It was required reading."

"Peaches says they're bad news, as in, we should avoid them."

"Your creature is correct in his assessment," Monty answered, without turning around. "We are in hostile territory. Make haste."

"Make haste? Who even says that anymore?"

"I do. Now move."

"I can't believe I'm suggesting this," I said, keeping pace. "Why don't we just teleport there?"

"That would attract undue attention," Monty said, walking fast. "The last thing we want in this place is attention. It would be best if we could enter and leave undetected...before nightfall."

"You mean, there's something out there that's worse than Dreadwolves?"

"Much worse," Monty said. "Using any ability would attract creatures I'd rather not face. Creatures that thrive on destruction and carnage."

"Oh, you mean the usual?"

"These are particular to this plane, and unpleasant."

"And they like to come out after dark?" I asked, jokingly. "What are they...runic roaches?"

"I believe my uncle called them 'The Unholy'," Monty answered. "In any case, I'm not eager to meet them. We need the Keep for its specific properties. We don't need to get into a confrontation here."

"I'm all for getting in and leaving without a fight," I said, looking around as we crossed the field. "This *is* Central Park."

"It's very likely that it is," Monty said. "Just not *our* Central Park."

"Our Central Park doesn't have boogeymen when the sun goes down," I said with a chuckle. "At least none that I know of."

"Precisely," Monty snapped. "The things we don't know, especially about this place, can end us. Move faster."

I had never seen Monty this nervous before. We had

picked up the pace to a brisk jog, when I noticed that the sun was setting.

"Monty?" I asked as the jog turned into a run. "The sun is going down. Why is the sun going down?"

"Our relation to time in this plane is compressing... that's inconvenient."

"You think?"

"Bloody hell," he said under his breath as he slowed. "We have company as well."

"Company? What kind of company? Dreadwolves?"

"To start," Monty said, gesturing as violet runes floated off into the air, "as well as something worse, and faster."

I drew Grim Whisper.

"What is it?" I said, looking into the distance behind us. "Can we stop it?"

"*We* aren't stopping anything...keep going," he said, stopping. "I'm going to slow down whatever may be after us."

"Wait, what?" I said, sliding to a halt. "What are you doing?"

"Go!" he yelled. "There are wards around the Keep. Get inside the wards. I'm right behind you."

I took off again with Peaches by my side, feeling the distinct sensation of having something chasing me. Ahead, the Keep looked marginally closer.

That's when I heard the growls.

<Bad dogs?>

<Yes and something else. Something very bad.>

<Try not to be so specific.>

<Bad dogs and other bad smells are coming.>

<We aren't going to fight them. Let's keep going to that building.>

<Maybe if you ate meat, you could run faster.>

<You have four legs, to my two. It's not fair.>

<They are getting closer. We will have to fight.>

<Can't we just run faster?>

<I can. Can you?>

<Try to keep...>

The thought evaporated as Peaches blasted off ahead of me. Clearly I was holding him back. I pumped my legs harder as the sounds of snarling surrounded me. Up ahead, Peaches had come to a stop.

In front of him stood the largest wolf I had ever seen. Peaches had taken a 'shred and maim' stance, but the only way he was going to intimidate this super wolf was to go XL.

"I am Fang," the large wolf said as he sniffed the air, surprising me because the voice wasn't in my head. "Alpha of this pack. Who...are...you?"

I noticed the sun was dipping below the horizon. It was getting darker by the second.

"My name is Simon and that"—I pointed to Peaches—"is Peaches, my bondmate."

Fang narrowed his eyes. Apparently, everyone except me had gone to glare school. He stared at me for a few seconds.

"Impossible. No creature of that power would bond with such a weakling," Fang said. "It's insulting."

"Listen, Cujo," I started, "there's no need to get snippy. We are just—"

"Seeking safe passage to the Hunter's Keep," Monty said, coming up behind me. "Well met, Fang of the Dreadwolves."

"We shall see," Fang said, looking at Monty and then

back at me. "You have ventured into my territory without passage."

"We're just passing through," I said. "If we knew there was a toll—"

"You are an insolent fool, to speak so," Fang said with a low growl. "How did you bond to this creature?"

"Simon," Monty said under his breath, before I could answer. "Measure your words."

"I don't know all of the details," I said, placing a hand on Peaches' head. "Probably because I'm awesome, and Peaches is a great judge of character."

"You named him...Peaches?" Fang asked, clearly upset. "He let *you* name him?"

"He didn't 'let me' do anything. He was named by a god," I said. "It's not like Fang is so original. What were the other choices? Mouse? Big Dog? Snarl?"

"Fang, because I sink them into the necks of those who oppose me...before I kill them," Fang answered with a snarl. "Tell me why I should let you live?"

"We are only seeking passage into the Hunter's Keep, and we mean you"—Monty glanced at me quickly—"no insult."

"You are not Hunters," Fang said, turning back to Monty, apparently done with me. "What business do you have in the home of the Hunters...our enemies?"

"I seek to spill no blood tonight," Monty said, letting his tone become menacing. "But if I must, yours will be the first."

"What happened to mean no insult?" I said under my breath. "You just threatened to spill the angry super wolf's blood? I'm really not in the mood to become dinner."

"It wasn't a threat," Monty said, staring at Fang.

Around us, several Dreadwolves had gathered. They looked eager to get started with their evening meal. I was guessing Monty would be the appetizer, since he only ate leaves. Peaches and I would be the main course. It wasn't a pleasant thought.

"Let me handle this," Monty muttered. "Before it escalates."

"Oh, I get it," I shot back under my breath. "This is *diplomacy*."

"We only seek peaceful passage," Monty said, ignoring me, "but will resort to violence if needed."

"This is not a land of peace," Fang said. "This is a land of death."

"Let's not start the evening with yours."

"Bold words, little man," Fang answered, with menace of his own. "On what name do you seek passage?"

Peaches had backed up next to me, still ready to pounce into shredding action. Monty formed a white hot orb of flame. It was radiating enough heat that I needed to take a few steps away from him.

"Overkill much?" I said, giving Monty space before I got a tan. "Do we plan on barbecuing them?"

Monty ignored me.

"I seek passage on the name of Tristan Montague, son of Connor Montague and nephew to Dexter Montague."

All of the Dreadwolves backed away, except Fang.

"I do not know you," Fang said, stepping forward with a low growl as I let my hand drift to the holster of Grim Whisper, "but the name of Dexter Montague is known to the pack. You may have safe passage to the Hunter's Keep...for tonight."

"I will let him know of your respect," Monty said.

"Do not fool yourself, Montague," Fang said. "We offer passage, but we do not respect you or your uncle."

If they didn't respect Monty or Dex, the driving force had to be fear. I glanced at the white orb floating gently in Monty's hand. Fear was a good choice.

"We will make haste to conclude our affairs in the shortest time possible."

"You would do well to conduct your business and leave this place, young Montague," Fang answered. "The Dread-wolves will honor the pact, but many of the Unholy in this land despise your name and your uncle."

"Understood," Monty said with a small bow. "We will not delay. Run long and fast."

"May the wind be always at your back," Fang replied with a nod, turning away. "Do not let the sun find you in our land."

I turned to see that the Dreadwolves had disappeared as quickly as they had appeared.

"That's odd," Monty said, absorbing the small sun he held in his hand. "That was much hotter than intended."

"Excuse me?" I asked. "What are you talking about?"

"Did that orb feel hotter than usual to you?"

"You mean the one that nearly barbecued my face?"

"So it did feel hotter?"

"Hotter than what? Sitting on the surface of the sun? It's not like I'm measuring the Kelvins of your orbs...that just sounded wrong."

"It seemed off," Monty said, pensively. "I didn't use more energy than usual."

A roar filled the park behind us.

"Sounds like our cue to get moving again," I said, jumping into a quick run behind Monty. "What is making that noise, by the way? I'm guessing it's not a Dreadwolf."

"You recall the ogres we've faced?"

"Do I have to?"

"That sound was made by a similar creature—at least in physiology."

"That didn't sound like any ogre we've faced," I said. "It sounded like an Ogre Plus on steroids."

"That is an apt description," Monty answered, veering slightly left as we approached the Keep. "It was the sound of a behemoth."

"Doesn't sound pleasant."

"It isn't," Monty added. "Behemoths are incredibly intelligent and formidable adversaries. It would be best to avoid them."

"That's why you were slowing down?"

"Yes, I placed a few traps to delay some of the more dangerous creatures in the park. The ones that posed the greatest threat."

"What was the whole thing with the lineage?" I asked. "For a second, I thought you were going to say, 'I'm Tristan Montague, from the clan Montague. In the end, there can be only one'. Sounded just like Connor McCloud."

"It sounds like you're pronouncing it 'McCloud' like clouds in the sky," Monty said. "I would imagine it would sound a little different since it's spelled 'MacLeod'. Probably closer to 'mac loud', just joined together."

"Do I look Scottish? You know it?"

"Who is Connor MacLeod?" Monty said, slowing down. "Is this some obscure reference from your movie-saturated brain?"

"Highlander? There can be only one? Are you serious?

With the great Sean Connery? Immortals fighting for a prize?"

"Are they?"

"Not that I know of, but this is Highlander."

"So you've said," Monty said, pacing and looking down. "Is it a movie about immortals?"

"Yes, Connor is from the highlands and he's taught by Sean Connery."

"And Sean teaches Connor the ways of the immortals, and how to fight?"

"Well, in the movie, he's Ramirez—"

"Ramirez? From the NYTF?"

"No," I said, glaring at him. "His character in the movie is named Ramirez. Sean plays a Spaniard."

"Let me see if I understand," Monty said. "You have an Irish Scot playing a Spaniard?"

"Yes, Sean is amazing in it."

"And he portrays a mentor who prepares the immortal highlander for the end...where there can only be one?" Monty asked. "That about right?"

"Yes! You've heard of it, then?"

"Doesn't ring a bell, sorry. Is it a travel movie about Scotland?"

"Did they ever let you out at the Golden Circle?"

"Of course we went out," Monty snapped. "We just didn't go out to the movies... we went out to war."

"I'll make sure you watch it when we get back. It's a classic."

"I think we have different definitions for the word, 'classic'," Monty said, as he stopped and crouched down. "We're here."

"The Keep is way over there," I said, looking across the field. "What are you talking about?"

He placed his hand on the ground and whispered a few words. The area surrounding us exploded with violet runes, delineating a large circle with the Keep in the center.

"Yes," Monty said, pointing down, "but the entrance is here."

FOUR

The runes formed a path straight to the now nearby Keep.

"It moved?" I said, looking at the fortress now several hundred feet away. "Teleportation?"

"A more likely explanation is that the distance compressed, like the bellows of an accordion, moving us closer to the Keep."

"This is what you meant by flexible distance," I said, looking around. "This doesn't look inviting in the least."

"It's not meant to be."

We walked the remaining distance to the massive door of the Keep.

It was an impressive, medium-sized fortress, complete with a corner turret and open-air pavilion. It bore a slight resemblance to Belvedere Castle—which existed in my Central Park—except the Hunter's Keep was squatter, angrier looking, and gave off an air of menace...like a predator ready to pounce.

"Are you sure no one lives here?" I asked, as we

followed the path. "B&E sounds like a bad idea in the land of Dreadwolves and worse."

"We are not breaking and entering," Monty said. "It's more like inviting ourselves in."

"Right," I said, looking around. "Is that behemoth going to catch up?"

"Not for a while. I added a time component to the trap," Monty said, approaching the massive door. "It will be stuck in a loop until we are done, unless it was something else."

"Something else?" I asked, concerned. "Care to elaborate?"

"Not particularly. Professor Ziller's treatise was far from conclusive. This is an entirely different plane. I doubt he could catalogue all of its denizens. Some of his research assistants never made it back from this plane."

"That's encouraging," I said, glancing back again. "Maybe we should hurry up?"

"This process can't be rushed," Monty said. "I have to examine the entrance first."

"So whatever made that noise could be a behemoth or something worse?"

"It's refreshing to see you're paying attention...for once."

"I'm not really enjoying this trip," I said, looking behind us. "Are you sure we can't do this test of yours on our home plane?"

"Quite," Monty said, touching the door and nodding. "There is a sequence. It's ancient, but functional."

"You seem to know plenty about this place," I said, looking around. "When was the last time you were here?"

"Uncle Dex brought me here during my first shift,"

Monty said, running his hand lightly over the door. "I don't remember much of it. My shift had rendered me mostly unconscious."

"Mostly...unconscious?" I said. "Maybe we should contact Dex, who I hope was fully conscious at the time?"

"He's busy at the Golden Circle, and we don't have that kind of time," Monty answered, focusing on the door. "You heard Fang, we are on a schedule, a limited one."

"We are not on a 'shedyul'," I corrected. "It's 'skedyul'."

"If we are here when the sun rises, it won't matter how it's pronounced," Monty said. "Even though 'shedyul' is the correct pronunciation."

"Why? What happens at sunrise? Do the reverse vampires flood the park?"

Monty just stared at me for a few seconds.

"Your brain is a disturbing place," he said and resumed examining the door. "At daybreak, the safe passage Fang extended expires."

"Shit," I said. "That sounds bad."

"The Dreadwolves will be the first to attack, followed by other sorts of elements from this plane," Monty said. "Before you ask, no, we can't teleport inside the wards surrounding the Keep. We have to physically be outside of the circle of wards to cast."

"Sounds like poor planning," I said. "I'm sure the hunter people had tunnels, or some other way to get out."

"Unlikely," Monty said, shaking his head. "A way out is also a way in."

"Good point. I wouldn't want to have another entrance to guard in this place," I said. "Did anyone inform these hunters that putting a base in enemy territory is a bad idea?"

"I think it was making a statement."

"What? Come and kill us?"

"We don't fear you, and we are dangerous enough to place our base of operations in your front yard."

I took a step back and admired the Hunters' Keep again. It did have a 'we are such badasses, we dare you to come knocking' feel to it. Still, it was foolish to put your HQ in the middle of hostile territory. It usually meant a short life span, no matter the statement being made.

"I can see the badassery of it, right up to the moment they get stormed and wiped out," I said. "By the way, what happened to the Hunters, if this place is empty?"

"My uncle is more knowledgeable on that subject," Monty answered, and placed a hand flat on the door. "I'm pretty certain I can figure this sequence out."

Monty positioned his face close to his hand, as if he were listening to a secret the door was sharing. I was hoping it was telling him to go home.

"'Pretty certain' doesn't give me much confidence in your ability to figure out an ancient set of runes," I said. "Why don't we just go back and visit Roxanne? Maybe she can find out what's wrong with me?"

"We will," Monty answered, with his head still against the door. "Right after we conduct the test."

"The words 'guinea pig' are coming to mind," I said. "Are you sure you don't just want to experiment on a phasing immortal?"

"I wouldn't undertake this test lightly," Monty answered, looking at me. "It would be dishonest to say I wasn't interested in the results. However, my first priority is to help you."

"Right, spoken like a true mad scientist or mad mage

in this case," I said. "Can you open that door before we get visitors who'd like to shred us?"

"If I weren't being distracted, this would be easier," Monty said, without turning to me. "Take in the architecture: a Keep of this age is a fascinating structure."

"Thanks, Frank Lloyd. I'm going to pass on the sightseeing if you don't mind."

"I don't, but I would prefer some quiet while I figure this out."

<Is the angry man hungry?>

<I don't know. Maybe, why?>

<He sounds hungry. If he ate meat he would be happy.>

<I don't think meat would make Monty happy. I don't know if anything could make him happy. He doesn't really do happy.>

<Should I lick him?>

<As much as I would like to see that, no, boy. That wouldn't make him happy. He's trying to concentrate on opening the door.>

<Can I help him?>

<Let's not. This isn't a place we want to redecorate. We have to go in and leave without damaging anything.>

<How do we do that?>

<Good question. You two have a habit of massive destruction.>

<My destruction only happens when I'm trying to help you. That means it's your fault.>

<That's some spin. Because I'm the one that tells you to go through walls and obliterate everything in your path?>

<Because as your bondmate, I will do everything to keep you safe. I'm not the one walking into danger, you are. I go where you go.>

My hellhound had just hit me with a deep zen

moment, and he was right. Time to try out the hellhound zen on the grumpy mage.

"Monty, why don't we call it a day...or night in this case?" I asked. "I mean, can't we go to Haven, let Roxanne run a few tests and deal with whatever it is?"

"We *will* do that."

"But you have to run your super dangerous test first, right?"

"Did you see my orb?"

"That sounds a little personal," I said. "I'm not paying attention to your orbs."

"Stop being foolish," he snapped. "The orb I cast earlier was affected by something other than my control."

"You're losing control?" I asked, warily. "What do you mean, exactly?"

"It was stronger than it should have been," he continued, "yet I didn't expend any additional energy."

"Maybe this place has extra ambient energy? It does have a certain *je ne sais quoi* of imminent destruction in the air."

"The runes back at the Moscow on my uncle's door, do you remember?"

"Yes, they were pulsing, I remember them."

"They never do that," Monty said, now staring at me. "Not in all the time that that door has contained runes have they pulsed like that."

"Are you saying the runes are broken?"

"They started pulsing when we got close," Monty answered, slowly as if thinking it through. "When *you* got close."

"What are you trying to say?" I asked, defensively. "Are you saying *I* broke the runes?"

"You can't 'break' runes by your mere presence," Monty replied. "You're not nearly that powerful. But it's possible that whatever is happening with your signature is responsible."

"Great," I said, throwing up a hand. "Now you're saying I'm runically radioactive?"

"I won't know for certain until I run the test. Please stand back," he said, waving me away from the door. "If something goes wrong—"

"Make it so nothing goes wrong."

"Don't be naive, Simon," he said. "If something can go wrong, it usually does. This door has an ancient rune set I'm trying to decipher under a time constraint. The odds of something going wrong are astronomically high."

"If something goes wrong," I said, "we'll deal with it like we always do."

"This is different," Monty said, keeping his voice low. "If I get this wrong, we could drop the wards around the Keep, or set off a failsafe that incinerates us where we stand. Both of those would be undesirable."

"That's one way to put it."

"I'm a mage, Simon," Monty said. "Mages don't do upbeat or"—he waved a hand—"motivational. We're realists. To be otherwise is delusional."

"It's not delusional to be optimistic once in a while," I countered. "Not everything is doom and gloom."

"We're standing in an alternate plane under the imminent threat of death," Monty replied. "Have you considered that you may not be immortal in this plane?"

"Excuse me?"

"The curse that ensures you remain alive after suffering some deadly attack may not function here," he said. "I don't know if Kali's influence extends to this or any other plane besides our own. We may very likely die here. That optimistic enough for you?"

"Montague Motivational Mornings," I said. "If you ever get tired of saving the world, you could start a course on how to get people to start their days. Feeling sluggish? Just imagine: your house could've blown up last night. Now go tackle the day!"

He stared at me for a few seconds and shook his head. I seem to have that effect on people.

"Just take a step over there...to the right," he said, pointing. "Stay out of the direct path of the door."

"I'll be careful," I said serious. "If I see anything weird, I'll react fast, maybe even take a jump to the left?"

"If you continue, I'll feed you to the Dreadwolves myself."

"Fine," I said, raising my hands in surrender and stepping over to the left, just so Monty understood I made my own choices, and away from the door. "Just bringing some much-needed humor."

"Your idea of humor gives me a migraine. Now let me focus."

He manipulated some of the runes, touching them in sequence. After a minute of careful selections, it looked like he was almost done.

"Did you crack it?"

"I believe so," Monty said. "This is the last rune in the sequence."

"You ready?" I asked, clearly not ready. "Are you sure?"

"No," Monty answered. "But when has that stopped us in the past?"

"Well, nothing ventured, nothing gained."

"Indeed," Monty said, pressing the last rune in the sequence. "That should do it."

Nothing happened.

"Did you break the door?" I asked, looking at the now dormant runes. "It seems to have stopped working."

"I'm pretty certain the sequence was"—he looked down—"bloody hell."

"The sequence was bloody hell? Since when did you start naming them?"

"The sequence was wrong," he said, angrily. "I somehow managed to bollocks it up."

That's when I knew we were in trouble. Monty rarely cursed, but when he did, it meant the situation had sailed past dire, and ended up squarely in 'oh shit' territory.

"What are you talking about?" I said, following his gaze to the ground. All of the ward runes that were previously violet had become black with a tinge of red. "I'm going to go out on a limb here and say *that* is not the desired effect?"

"Not in the least," Monty said, as he began gesturing. "The wards around the Keep have been inverted."

"Inverted? You mean—?"

"Instead of keeping everything out," he said, pointing to the ground. "These wards are now a beacon for everything in this park to head our way."

Howls and roars filled the night.

"Oh, shit."

FIVE

There was a stark border where the wards ended around the Keep.

"When you say 'everything', what exactly—?"

"I mean everything," Monty said. "Starting with the Dreadwolves."

I drew Grim Whisper. I didn't materialize Ebonsoul because I didn't know what we were going to face. Plus, Ebonsoul required proximity. I had a feeling keeping my distance from whatever was coming, was going to be important.

I changed the magazine to entropy rounds. Somehow, the idea of persuader rounds being effective in this place seemed like a joke. Besides, if something was coming to tear me apart, the only persuading I wanted to do involved immediate disintegration...theirs, not mine.

"Can't we just blast our way into the Keep? How strong is that door?"

Monty took a step back and assessed the door of the Keep.

"This door makes the doors at the Randy Rump appear inconsequential," he said. "The stones of the Keep itself are vibrating with power. I'd judge blasting of any sort would be a futile exercise, unless we possessed the equivalent of a runic nuclear device. In which case, if we did detonate such a device, we'd be the first casualties."

"Is that a no?"

"A profound one," Monty said. "This is a base in enemy territory. At the very least, they would invest heavily in the security of the Keep, starting with the doors. If there is a material harder than runed Buloke Ironwood, this is it."

"Okay then, no blasting," I said going over options. "Can we teleport out of here?"

"If I'm not mistaken, we are currently trapped inside the ward circle," Monty said, pointing at the ground. "The wards will prevent us from leaving the Keep, at least until the creatures of this place eliminate us."

"Basically, we can check out anytime we like, but we can never leave?"

"These specific wards seem to inhibit egress of any kind," Monty said, narrowing his eyes and looking at the ground, "with unpleasant side effects."

"Including teleportation?"

"That is my working theory," Monty said, tracing violet runes in the air. "The wards will prevent that particular casting...I think."

"But you aren't sure," I said, looking down at the black and red runes. "Let's find out."

"Nothing is certain in this plane, except that we will have a violent confrontation shortly."

"Maybe we can get out before then?" I asked. "I'm going to test your working theory."

"Feel free," he said, shaking his head. "I'm going to prepare for the impending conversation."

"Somehow I don't think Fang and his crew will want to discuss much this time around," I said, walking over to the edge of the ward circle with Peaches by my side. "Especially after that whole 'spill your blood' comment. I'm sure he appreciated that."

"The comment was necessary," Monty said. "Dreadwolves can smell fear."

"They must've smelled me from across the park," I said, looking down at the runes. "These things look nasty by the way."

Peaches nudged me in the leg, nearly launching me across the threshold of runes and dislocating my hip.

<*You need to recalibrate your nudges.*>

<*How would I do that? More meat?*>

<*Have you ever heard that less is more?*>

<*With meat, more is more.*>

<*We need to see how bad these wards are.*>

He sniffed the wards under us and chuffed.

<*They are bad. Is this one of those times you are going to get into trouble?*>

<*No, boy. I'm just going to make sure these runes are really trapping us. It would be crazy to stay here if we aren't trapped.*>

<*It would be crazy to stay here even if we are. This place is bad.*>

<*No argument from me. Stay right here at the edge. I'm going to pass the edge of the wards and see what happens.*>

<*That doesn't sound like a good idea.*>

<*I'm just going to check if we are really trapped in this place.*>

He gave off a low whine and crouched down.

"Stop being so dramatic," I said, stepping over the edge of the wards. "See it's not so—"

A burning sensation raced up my leg followed by the extreme feeling of pins and needles, as if my foot had fallen asleep. The next moment, I was airborne and heading to the stone wall of the Keep at speed.

A blast of air deflected my trajectory, preventing my face from smashing into the stone. I bounced on the ground hard and rolled several feet, and coming to a stop some distance from the Keep.

"Satisfied?" Monty asked. "Or would you like to try again?"

Peaches padded over to where I lay, ready to unleash a slobber attack.

"I'm good," I said, waving an arm and nudging him away. "Couldn't you form a gentle cushion of air, instead of bouncing me like a handball all over the place?"

"I did," Monty answered. "It seems that whatever is affecting you is also affecting any casting around you."

"Are you sure it's not this place?" I said, standing with a groan. "My everything hurts."

"No, I'm not," Monty answered. "Still in pain?"

"Yes," I said, rubbing my elbow. "That wasn't exactly my idea of a graceful landing, you know."

"You're not understanding. Are you still in pain?"

"I just answered you...yes. What—is my voice not carrying over to where you are?"

"I'm hearing you just fine," Monty snapped. "I'm just wondering."

"Wondering what?" I replied with the same snappish tone. "Am I not speaking proper English?"

"That's a given," Monty answered. "I'm wondering... shouldn't your healing kick in after any damage?"

"Of course. Except—"

"It didn't?"

"It didn't," I said, the realization slowly dawning on me. "The only time the pain lingers is when I meet with Karma. When I'm—"

"Mortal?"

"This is bad, Monty. I'm not in the mood to die in a fake Central Park today."

"Or any other day, I would hope," Monty said, dropping more violet runes around us. They floated gently for a second and then disappeared into the ground. "I'd advise extra caution in our upcoming confrontation."

"Good advice," I said, nodding. "These behemoths you mentioned earlier, do they look like ogres that've been turned into boulders, about ten feet tall and half as wide? Something like mountains of angry scariness?"

"I'd say that's accurate," Monty replied, pausing the rune creation. "Wait, you've never encountered a behemoth. Do you see one?"

"No."

"Good, they are unpleasant, dangerous—"

"I see two," I said, pointing to the other side of Keep. "They don't look happy to see us."

The behemoths were headed our way...fast.

SIX

"Which way?" Monty asked. "Where do you see them?"

"They're just like ogres, right?"

The behemoths stood over ten feet tall, with hands the size of dinner plates. It was like looking at a mutant Ben Grimm come to life, except they weren't orange and the only thing fantastic about these things was how fast they were moving.

"Wrong," Monty said, creating more runes. "Behemoths are intelligent creatures of massive destruction. Ogres are mindless engines of destruction, following instinct. Behemoths are cognitively superior, despite their outward appearance. Do not let them fool you."

"Their appearance tells me they're here to welcome us to the park by ripping off an arm or two, then engaging in vigorous stomping."

Monty stepped around the Keep to get a better look at the enormous creatures of impending death heading our way.

"That's odd," he said, peering into the night. "They

usually run in large groups. Two seems like a feint. I thought there'd be more than that."

I turned to stare at him.

"Don't sound so disappointed," I said. "I'm sure there's more out there somewhere. Do you know how to stop them?"

"Aim high," Monty said, reaching behind his back and drawing the Sorrows as they materialized in his hands. "The head."

"Tell me you aren't about to say what I think you're about to say," I groaned. "The head?"

I holstered Grim Whisper.

"To paraphrase the inimitable Ramirez," Monty said over the wailing of his swords. "If the head comes away from the neck, it's over."

"You do know who he is!"

"I was talking about the head of the NYTF," Monty answered. "Who are you referring to?"

"Never mind," I said, knowing he would never admit he understood my reference. "This is like trying to ace the Kobayashi Maru. It's a no-win scenario."

"Then we need to change the rules of engagement," he answered, swinging his swords once again. "Turn a no-win scenario into one we can win."

"Have I ever told you how creepy those swords are?" I asked. "Why do they wail like that?"

"They're named the Sorrows for a reason," he said, letting energy flow into the blades. They gave off a blue glow as he extended his arms. "Rumor has it that each blade is forged with the life of a sylph."

"What's the Zillerplanation?"

"The energy channeled through the blade causes air to

be displaced over the surface as it moves through space. This displacement produces an auditory effect. The sounds you hear as wails."

Monty swung the blades in the air. Each practice cut he executed, sounded like the weeping of a young girl. Black runes covered the silver blades on both sides. The hilt was the figure of a young woman with her arms outstretched to the sides. When Monty extended the sword, the figure's arms wrapped loosely around his wrist, forming a guard.

"Will they work against the boulders headed our way?" I asked, eyeing the behemoths closing in on us. "As in, can you stop them?"

"Only one way to find out," he said, with a few more practice swings. "They are Seraphs after all."

"'Only one way to find out?'" I said, incredulously. "How about something a little more positive? You know, like: "'These Seraphs will absolutely obliterate those behemoths, Simon.'"

"I don't know if that's true," Monty answered. "Why would I make such an unproven claim?"

"Because it would make me feel better?"

"Ah, I see," Monty replied. "Never fear, Simon. The Sorrows will be quite effective in delaying the behemoths from ripping your arms off for at least five to ten minutes. Better?"

"Not even close," I said. "Your pep talks suck."

"The Seraphs *should* be strong enough," Monty added, "even in this plane."

"Seraphs are for demons," I said. "I don't know what classification behemoths belong to, but I doubt it's demons."

"True," Monty answered, "However the properties that make them Seraphs, imbue them with more power than any ordinary, or even runed, blade. I daresay we have the advantage, as long as we can avoid their fists."

"Even with all of our blades, I think they may have the slight edge here."

"Lack of immortality aside, you have your weapons. I'm a mage with considerable ability—even though said ability is questionable right now—and we have your creature that can certainly challenge them. The odds are about even."

"Can you stop trying to cheer me up?"

"Was I successful?"

"Not in the slightest," I said. "What's the plan?"

"Don't die."

"Great plan. Not complicated at all."

"Simple plans are the best plans."

The behemoths had reached the edge of the wards and stopped. It looked like they were having second thoughts about crossing the threshold. Behind them, in the distance, I saw the first pack of Dreadwolves. This was getting worse by the second.

We were going to need some industrial-sized help.

"Why did they stop?" I asked under my breath, keeping my eyes on the two angry mountains. "They look confused."

"They probably don't realize the wards are down...yet," Monty answered. "I'm sure that situation will be rectified shortly."

<*Hey, boy. You see those large creatures over there?*>

<*They smell bad.*>

<I bet they do. I'm going to need you to go XL on them before they stomp us.>

<Will the angry man make me extra meat? I haven't eaten in so long.>

<You ate this morning, a few hours ago.>

<But now it's night time. That is a long time.>

<Fine. I'll make sure Monty makes you extra meat. We'll even go to the place and get you your favorite meat.>

<I'm going to need a larger meat portion. Frank says never settle for a little when you can get more. Two bowls, please.>

<Frank said? Tell you what, when Frank is making meat for you, he can negotiate how much you get. Until then, one bowl.>

<This sounds like more of your fasting punishment.>

<Any second now, those two are going to figure out they can cross into this area. I don't want to get crushed today. Can you convince them that smashing us is a bad idea?>

<Yes. You will have to move away.>

<Thank you. I'll speak to Monty about your meat.>

<Thank you. I'm starving.>

<You haven't starved a day in your life.>

I stepped away from Peaches as he bowed his head and growled. Monty glanced behind me and nodded.

"Battle mode?" he asked. "A good idea...considering."

"He tried to negotiate for two bowls of meat...because, Frank."

"Two bowls? You may need to place him on a diet of meat, and of Frank," Monty said, looking back at my hellhound, "although I haven't noticed any measurable difference in his weight."

"Don't encourage him," I said. "He's getting too heavy."

A deep rumbling sound vibrated along the ground and

in the pit of my stomach. The runes along Peaches' flanks exploded with red energy as the air around him became charged with power.

"Perhaps a bit more space is required," Monty said, stepping away. "He does get quite large."

Peaches spread his forelegs, sinking several inches into the ground. He shook his body and barked, nearly bursting my eardrums in the process as his eyes gleamed red. My ears were still ringing as he grew, reaching battle-mode size.

The behemoths turned to look at the new Peaches XL and then back at me.

"What are you doing?" Monty asked as I approached the edge of the ward circle. "I don't think they'll be up for a chat that doesn't involve grinding you to dust."

The behemoths towered above me, looking down. I couldn't make out their facial expressions. It would be like trying to figure out if a rock was smiling. What I could tell from their body language is that they wanted to share vast amounts of pain with me.

"You always say we should try diplomacy," I said, keeping out of arms reach. "I'm going to convince them to go home."

"Are you now?" Monty asked. "How do you intend to do that?"

"Tactful negotiation...watch."

Monty said they were intelligent. I was about to find out just how intelligent they were.

"You two should head back where you came from," I said, letting the silver mist of Ebonsoul coalesce into the blade in my hand. "We don't want any trouble, and I would hate to have to kill you."

"You have some power," Boulder One said on the right. "It won't be enough to keep you alive. Cross the threshold. We will end you quickly."

"You?" Boulder Two said, with what I can only imagine was a laugh, but sounded closer to gravel being crushed. "Kill us? With what? That little knife?"

I nodded.

"With my little knife, the angry mage, and my very large bondmate back there," I hooked a thumb behind me, pointing at Peaches. "He would love to chew on you, even though you probably taste horrible."

"Your bondmate and your wizard matter little," Boulder One said, slowly stepping backward from the edge of the ward circle. "You have entered our land and you will die."

I stepped back to where Monty stood bristling.

"Did he just call me a wizard?" Monty asked.

"Caught that, did you?" I said. "To be honest, it's a little hard to tell all you magic types apart."

"I am not a wizard."

"One sec," I said, raising a finger, "before you start the magerant."

<Hey boy, that behemoth is going to test the defenses and find them missing. You should probably convince him that would be a mistake.>

<I WILL PREEMPTIVELY INTERCEPT HIS TRAJECTORY TO DISSUADE HIM FROM THIS COURSE OF ACTION.>

<What do you mean preemptively intercept? Just let him know—>

I was mid-thought when Peaches bounded towards the incoming behemoth. The ground shook with each step he took. Peaches met Boulder One at the edge of the ward circle headfirst and launched him back several hundred feet...well most of him. Parts of the behemoth flew off in several directions at once from the impact.

Boulder Two turned on Peaches, swinging a fist at my hellhound.

<PLEASE COVER YOUR EARS.>

"Monty, ears!"

Monty reabsorbed the Sorrows and gestured in one smooth motion as Peaches backed up, inhaled and barked. A sphere formed around Monty and me as Boulder Two received the full brunt of the barkwave. I noticed Peaches had stepped outside the ward circle, without being launched back towards the Keep.

Even with the sphere of silence around us, I could feel the vibration of his bark tremble the ground beneath us. Boulder Two never stood a chance. The bark punched into and through the behemoth with extreme force, blasting it to rubble.

"I don't remember your creature being this powerful," Monty said, dropping the sphere. "It would seem that whatever is affecting you has influenced his power level as well."

<THE MAGE'S ASSESSMENT IS CORRECT. I SENSE AN EXPONENTIAL INCREASE IN THE POWER LEVEL I AM CURRENTLY EXHIBITING. THIS IS NOT THE NORM AND IT WILL REQUIRE LARGER DOSES OF SUSTENANCE TO MAINTAIN THIS FORM.>

<That just sounds like a sneaky way to say you need more meat.>

<IF I AM TO REMAIN IN THIS FORM FOR A

PROLONGED AMOUNT OF TIME, I WILL NEED TWICE THE AMOUNT OF SUSTENANCE.>

<Nice try. How about you get out of battle mode for now? I don't want something happening and keeping you stuck in XL mode because of this place.>

<AS YOU WISH.>

A few seconds later, Peaches returned to normal size. The transition back to normal size usually took a little longer and now I was getting worried that this place wasn't just affecting me, it was doing something to him as well.

Even worse, he was outside the ward circle and I was stuck inside. I stepped to the edge again and tried to extend my hand passed the threshold, only to feel the air solidify in front of me.

Peaches bounded back into the ward circle.

<How did you do that?>

<Do what? Break the rock men? My bark is strong.>

<No, go out of the circle and then come back in without a problem.>

<I'm strong because I eat meat. If you ate more meat, you could leave that circle too.>

<I don't think that's it actually. Let me try something.>

<Are you going flying again?>

<Not if I can help it.>

"Monty, can we try something?" I asked, walking to the edge of the ward circle. "I need to test a theory."

"You realize we have packs of Dreadwolves, more behemoths, and worse headed this way?"

"I do," I said, looking out into the night. "This might explain some things. Humor me."

"What is it?" Monty snapped. "What is this theory, and

what makes it so pressing that it needs to be tested now of all times?"

"Can you try and cross the ward circle threshold?"

"I told you we're trapped," Monty said. "Whatever I did to that door inverted the runes."

"What if it wasn't you?"

"What are you trying to say?" Monty asked. "That *you* somehow caused this?"

"Yes," I said with a nod. "Give it a try. What's the worst that can happen? It launches you back to the Keep? Create an air pillow."

More howls filled the night.

"This is a futile exercise," Monty answered, exasperated. "But if it will get you to focus on the imminent threat rushing towards us, fine."

He stepped over the ward circle threshold.

Nothing happened.

SEVEN

"Bloody hell," Monty said, standing outside of the ward circle. "How is this possible?"

"Does this mean I'm trapped here?"

"It would appear so," Monty said, stepping back into the circle. "We need to get into that Keep. It may be your only way out of this plane."

"We may want to deal with them first," I said, looking behind him. "They don't look ready to let us go anywhere."

Fang approached the edge of the circle.

"Montague, he is ours," Fang said. "The weak one bound to the hound of power belongs to us."

"I don't belong to anyone," I said raising my voice. "Go home."

"Prove it, weakling," Fang said. "Step out of the circle."

"I'm not in the mood right now. I like it in here."

"Of course you do," Fang answered. "Because you can't leave."

"What do you mean 'he is yours'?" Monty asked. "He is not a Dreadwolf."

“He is tainted,” Fang answered. “I can smell it on him.”

“I just forgot to put on deodorant this morning,” I said, raising my arms and smelling my pits. “Nothing a shower can’t fix.”

“This smell is beyond your body, weak—”

“The name is Simon, not weakling,” I said, interrupting him. “If you’re so powerful, why don’t you come in here?”

Fang stepped forward and crossed into the ward circle. The runes around him glowed red as his fur began to smolder.

“I am powerful enough to withstand these effects for a short time,” Fang said, as his body began to smoke. “Soon, this will happen to you...Simon, the weakling.”

Fang slowly backed out of the circle and the smoking stopped. I wasn’t feeling any warmer, but that didn’t look comfortable at all.

“How?” I asked. “I’m not even from this plane.”

“It matters not,” Fang said with a growl. “Either you come to us or we will take you.”

“You will not,” Monty said, standing in front of me. “He belongs to no one but himself, and maybe a particularly dangerous vampire.”

“Gee, thanks,” I said from behind Monty. “Chi doesn’t own me either, you know.”

“If you need to keep telling yourself that, I understand.”

“It doesn’t matter, Montague. He will never leave this place...alive,” Fang answered, retreating into the shadows. “Either the Keep will kill him or the Blights will. We will be ready when the fire begins to consume you, weakling.”

“Blights?” I asked, looking at Monty as the Dreadwolves disappeared. “What the hell are blights?”

"I don't know," Monty said, heading back to the Keep door. "I've never heard of them."

"Wonderful," I said. "Have I mentioned what a bad idea this whole trip has been?"

"You may have alluded to that sentiment once or twice," Monty said, drawing one of his Sorrows. "This requires drastic measures."

"Drastic measures?" I asked, concerned. "What are you doing? Put that sword away."

"I can't use your blade," Monty said, focusing on the door. "It's a siphon. This is the only way."

"Hold on a second," I answered. "Usually when someone says 'this is the only way' it means they don't want to try any other option, not that there aren't any."

"We need to get this door open before you start incinerating. This is the only way."

"I'm a huge fan of not becoming a smoked sausage, but I'm not liking the tone here," I said, holding up both hands. "What are you doing with your sword?"

"Saving you."

"No, Monty. Not like this. We can find another way."

Monty walked past the edge of the ward circle. He drew his sword across his forearm, drawing blood. The blood floated over to his hand as he gestured.

"Step away from the door, Simon. This may have some nasty side effects. I realize now what is keeping this place sealed."

"You mean the big ass door behind me?" I asked. "Take a picture of the runes and let someone decipher them. Maybe Professor Ziller can figure them out?"

"I figured them out," Monty said. "The entire Keep is under a blood ward. This is why conventional methods didn't work. The blood ward prevents me from accessing the runes."

"You don't know that for sure," I said, trying to convince him. "You could have just made a mistake. It has been known to happen."

"This is *not* a mistake," he shot back, raising his voice. "The blood ward must have somehow sensed something within you. This is why you're trapped in the circle. It could very well be your curse."

"Okay, it could be my curse," I said calmly. Clearly this plane was getting to all of us. "Using blood magic isn't going to improve the situation. How about you go back to our plane, find some bigger mage brains and ask them how to reverse this blood ward."

"I know how to reverse a blood ward," he said, gesturing again. "Like this."

The blood in his hand formed a large rune and floated over to the door. It sank into the wood and disappeared. The door burst with red light, and shot out a beam of energy. The beam slammed into Monty and latched onto his wound.

"What is that?" I yelled. "Stop this Monty!"

"Apparently, it needs more blood than I anticipated," Monty said, falling to his knees. "When the door opens, get inside and send your creature for help. That should get you off this plane safely."

"What are you talking about?" I said, looking from Monty to the door. "You need to stop this."

He was still outside the circle, which meant I couldn't reach him. I ran for the door and plunged Ebonsoul into the origin of the tether. The door erupted with energy, severing the tether and knocking me away, towards the edge of the ward circle.

I saw Peaches running to me and then blinking out. I was moving too fast for him to catch. I slammed into the ward circle wall, and the world became black.

EIGHT

I opened my eyes in a large hospital bed.

It reminded me of Haven, and I expected to see an angry Roxanne drift into view any second to chastise me for doing something dangerous and ending up in her care...again.

That's when I noticed the ceiling. Unless Roxanne had renovated Haven to medieval modern, I didn't think the ceiling would be made of stone.

We were inside the Keep.

"You're awake. Good," a female voice said. "I take it your friend was the one who attempted to undo the blood ward?"

I nodded, finding my throat too dry to speak. I sat up and looked around. Focusing on the room was difficult when it was slowly moving away from me and tilting. I lay my head back and closed my eyes for a few seconds until the sensation of moving passed.

"This feels almost as bad as teleportation," I mumbled. "Where am I?"

"You're in the Hunter's Keep," the woman said. "Which is, in the best of circumstances, difficult. Now, under a blood ward, it's nearly impossible."

"Did you happen to notice my stomach on the ground outside somewhere doing flip flops?"

"Here, drink this," she said, handing me a cool glass of water. "You're experiencing side effects from forcibly severing a tether. Actually, you didn't really sever it, it just jumped hosts. From your friend to you. Were you trying to kill yourselves?"

"We were trying to get inside," I rasped. "He thought bypassing the blood ward was the best way."

"To end his life, perhaps," she said. "I'm Calisto. You're lucky I came out when I did. Or both of you would've been gone. You, actually, should be dead."

I looked around and saw an unconscious Monty laying in a bed next to mine. Calisto didn't dress like a doctor. She wore casual hiking clothes, a brown t-shirt, dark jeans, and black hiking boots. Her long brown hair was pulled back into a loose ponytail.

"Normally, I would say that's easier said than done," I answered. "But this place has me feeling off. I'm Simon, and that's"—I pointed over to Monty—"Tristan."

She looked rugged, like a woman that felt more at home outdoors, in the mountains, not in a stone fortress. I looked around for my hellhound, but the bear was blocking my view of that side of the room.

That's when my brain registered the enormous bear.

"I must've hit my head really hard somewhere," I said, trying to focus on the other side of the room and failing. "That's the only thing that would explain the large bear illusion I'm seeing."

"That's not an illusion," Calisto said, turning to look back at the enormous polar bear sitting by the door next to my hellhound. "That's my bear, Ursados. He's my friend and a gate."

Ursados was the largest polar bear I'd ever seen. Not that I was an authority on bear sizes. Next to him, Peaches appeared to be a miniature hellhound.

"A gate?"

"Ursados is the only way to navigate a blood ward like the one around this Keep," Calisto said. "Without his ability, trying to get past the door is like reading a book, threading a needle, and sharpening a blade, all at once. The result is usually a bloody mess."

"That sounds about right," I said, rubbing my head. "Monty said this place was deserted. You live here?"

"Live, is a strong term," Calisto said. "I'm bound to the park. Why didn't you use your animal?"

"Use Peaches?" I asked. "I don't understand."

"He's a gate, isn't he? He certainly feels like one. He must be quite powerful. Ursados doesn't usually get along with other animals. He seems to like your Peaches."

"I never thought of Peaches that way, but you're right--he can go in-between planes."

"Like I said, a gate. Now let's get to the real issue. Why are you here?"

I explained Monty's theory about my energy signature and how I may be dying. I even told her what Fang said about my being tainted and being one of them.

"You met Fang?" she asked. "And survived?"

"Twice even, along with two behemoths," I added. "Peaches took care of those."

"Alone? He is strong. Very few would dare to face one behemoth alone, much less two."

"He's much stronger than he looks, as long as there's sausage to be had," I said. "The behemoths were a little dicey though. I'd never seen one of those."

Calisto looked over to where Peaches sat.

"He's not a Dreadwolf, but he's not an ordinary animal either. How did you find each other?"

"I don't think you'd believe me even if I told you," I said. "He was given to me by the god of the underworld."

"I see," Calisto said, seeming to take it in stride. "Can you communicate with Peaches?"

"Yes," I said. "We're bonded."

"That explains the connection I sense," Calisto said. "How about your wizard friend? I can tell he wields power."

"Mage, not wizard. He gets touchy about the title."

"Mages usually are," she said with a nod, looking at Monty. "Fang was mistaken. You're not tainted."

"I'm not?" I asked. "Why couldn't I leave the circle of wards."

"You have several bonds happening at once," Calisto said. "Your energy signature isn't tainted, it's scrambled. You're a mess. I sense no less than three powerful bonds happening simultaneously. Two seem clear, or at least getting there, but that last one...you need help."

"That last bond? How bad?"

"Beyond anything I've ever seen. It didn't seem like a bond at all. More like a curse."

"That would be right," I said. "I'm hellbound, blade-bound and cursed alive."

"What blade?" she asked, looking around. "I see no weapon besides your gun."

I focused and let the silver mist form in my hand. A moment later, I held Ebonsoul. Its dark blade glistened in the light. The runes that made it a Seraph gave off a soft red glow.

"This blade."

"That is an exceptional weapon," Calisto said. "Did you forge this?"

"No, it was given to me."

"By an enemy?"

"An enemy? No," I said, surprised. "Why would an enemy give me a weapon?"

"That"—she said, pointing at Ebonsoul—"is a dark blade. It radiates darkness, blood-thirst, and death. Whoever gave you that weapon did not give you a gift. They gave you a curse."

I thought about Ebonsoul, and how Monty said I had a habit of attracting nastiness. Now I wondered if it was me attracting the chaos in my life, or if it was Ebonsoul? Did Chi know what she was giving me when she gave me the blade?

"That's not what's wrong with you though," Calisto replied. "You're out of place."

"I feel like I'm all here," I said, patting myself down. "What do you mean?"

"You're shifting with reality."

"Monty said I was dying," I answered. "He wasn't positive, which is why we're here."

"Shifting would seem like dying to the untrained eye," Calisto replied, glancing at Monty. "No, what I mean is that you're acting like an open gate. You're out of phase.

That's why the Keep reacted to you, and why you couldn't leave the ward circle."

"How did this happen?" I asked. "Overexposure to runic energy?"

"What? No," she corrected. "This is a temporal disturbance."

"A disturbance," I said pensively. "Like a disturbance in the force?"

"I don't know what you mean by 'the force'," Calisto answered. "This is a temporal situation."

"Does it happen often?"

"I've never seen a case like yours, but I've seen it occurring with time-skippers," she said. "You don't seem like a time-skipper. No offense, but you don't possess enough power to stop time."

"None taken. What happens to time-skippers?"

"When they leap around time, they cause ripples," Calisto said, bringing her hands together and then spreading them apart. "After a while, the ripples bounce back creating causal anomalies."

She must have seen the expression on my face.

"Right," I said. "Can you pretend I didn't understand a word you just said?"

"Forgive me," Calisto said. "These subjects can become quite complex. In simple terms, a causal anomaly is the same as being rejected by time. Those around the anomaly, experience causal disruptions."

"What if I could stop time?" I asked. "Not for long, but for a few seconds at a time?"

"Then that would explain what's happening to you," Calisto answered, her voice grim. "Your disruption of time is causing your reality to be impacted. Every time you time-skipped, you splintered your timeline, creating parallels."

"Times when I didn't time-skip or made other choices?"

"Exactly. Over time—pardon the pun, this creates a temporal backlash. You become out of phase, causing anomalies around you."

"What kind of anomalies?"

"At first, it will be small things. Time dilations or hiccups. Lose a minute here or there. You barely realize it. Then it gets progressively worse."

"Worse how?"

"You start to impact cause and effect," she said. "Things won't work the way they should. There would be either magnifications of power or a complete absence. It's hard to tell."

"Because the cases are rare?"

"Well, that, and the subjects usually implode or are lost in time streams, never to return. Time will, and does, balance. No one escapes it for long."

"Has anyone been cured of the time ripples?" I asked. "Can it be stopped?"

"Of course," Calisto said with a nod. "The quickest way is with a blade."

"I meant a non-lethal method," I said. "Can they be reversed?"

"I've never heard of that," Calisto said. "Now you're getting into territory that is beyond me. I would imagine you'd need to undo whatever gave you the ability to skip time in the first place?"

"That sounds complicated."

"True," she said. "I really don't know if it's possible.

Death seems to be a sure fire method, though."

"Will Monty be okay?" I asked, glancing his way. "He's looking a little pale."

"You probably saved his life by jumping into the tether. He'll recover soon. Wizards are a hardy bunch. You, on the other hand, should be a corpse."

"Can he still run his test?" I asked. "He wanted to see what exactly was wrong with me."

"Yes. Once he recovers, and provided it doesn't involve blood magic of any kind," Calisto answered. "If he can agree to that then he's free to conduct his test."

"What happens if it contains blood magic?" I asked, because living dangerously was my middle name.

"Blood magic outside of the Keep will trigger a neutralizing effect, like the tether."

"What happens inside?"

"I wouldn't be able to get to you in time. You'd be wiped out before you could blink."

"Right. No blood magic. Noted."

"Good plan," she said. "I'll be back shortly. I need to reset the wards your friend inverted."

"Will that let me leave the ward circle?"

"Not while you're alive, no. I hope the test your friend wants to run can help you find a way out of here. If not, you're stuck."

NINE

"Can we run the less painful version of the test now that we know what we're dealing with?" I asked, as Monty created runes in the air around me. "Something like the torture-lite version?"

"I appreciate you stepping into the tether," Monty said, as he kept tracing runes in the air. "Thank you."

"You're welcome," I said. "Glad to keep you around, even if you're still grumpy."

"Surviving the tether means you're still somewhat immortal, which is good."

"I'd like to think so," I said. "I'm kind of used to breathing."

"We still need to run the test," Monty replied. "It's the only way to determine if what Calisto said is correct."

"She seems pretty trustworthy. I think we can take her at her word."

"We can't," he said. "You even said so yourself. She feels out of her depth with your condition."

"What about Sid?" I asked, suddenly remembering a

pain-free option. "Maybe he could help? It seems like this would be his area of expertise."

"Of course. Sid," Monty said. "Why didn't I think of him? Do you have his number?"

"Well, no."

"How exactly should I reach out to him? Does he have a special signal I could light up the night sky with?"

"Oh, hilarious," I replied. "Really?"

"Maybe he lives in a manor with a butler, and beneath, he has a convenient secret cave base of operations no one knows about?" Monty asked. "Do you have the cave address? We could head over there immediately."

"You really have missed your calling. For the record, we do *not* mock the Bat."

"Do you think Sid is really Batman?" Monty asked with feigned seriousness. "Are you sure his name isn't Bruce?"

"How much blood did you lose from that tether?" I asked. "Sounds like not enough is reaching your brain."

"Do you hear how preposterous your suggestion sounds?" Monty retorted. "You want me to reach out to someone who, what did you say he was, oh yes, I recall...a designer."

"That's what *he* said he was," I answered. "A Lead Designer."

"What exactly does this Sid *design*?"

"Streams, specifically time streams."

"A time stream designer," Monty said, nodding. "When you saw him, was there a large blue telephone box nearby?"

"What? No," I said. "I was inside the Randy Rump waiting for you when he came in."

"Did he show you a specific device, something sonic? A screwdriver, perhaps?"

"All he gave me was the box," I said, slightly upset. "I showed it to you, if you remember."

"Of course, the keepsaker," Monty said, with a nod. "Did James manage to see him? Anyone else?"

"Are you saying I imagined Sid?"

"No, I'm asking if anyone else saw him enter the Randy Rump when he appeared."

"Don't think so. He kind of stopped time when he appeared."

"Well, that's convenient," Monty said. "How exactly are we supposed to contact Sid, the Lead Designer of time streams?"

"I didn't contact him at all. He just showed up. You're the mage. I thought you'd have some idea, seeing as he sounds like he belongs more to *your* world than mine."

"My world *is* your world," Monty said. "You do realize we're having this conversation in an alternate plane? Your idea of normal left the station without you long ago, Chosen of Kali."

"No need to rub it in," I groused. "I'm aware of how different my life is, trust me."

"I do," Monty answered. "With my life."

"But we still have to run the test, don't we?"

Monty nodded.

"I'm not refuting that there are entities out there that may indeed manage time streams," Monty said. "There could be an entire organization of *designers* devoted to the time streams alone. Just your suggestion to call him *now*, in order to avoid an excruciating energy signature test is futile. I wouldn't know where to start. Would you?"

"I don't know," I snapped, frustrated. "He gave me the

keepsaker and called it purpose, a ripple in the pond. That was about as clear as a mage."

"Did you open it?" Monty asked. "At least to see what this Sid person was trying to say?

"No," I said. "In fact, I still have it in one of my"—I patted my pockets—"in one of my...wait, here."

I pulled out the keepsaker box that Sid had given me.

"Open it," Monty said. "At least that way we can put this entire Sid topic behind us."

"The last time I tried to, I nearly sprained a wrist," I said, handing the small box to Monty. "It was sealed tight. You try."

Monty examined the keepsaker closely, turning it in his hand and shook his head.

"This is covered in runes particular to you," he said. "Did you know that?"

"Hello? Not a mage. My runic reading is basic at best, which is dangerous on a good day. How do you know?"

"Some of these characters allude to a 'Chosen of Kali' who steps out of time," Monty replied, still turning the box. "Sound like anyone you know?"

"Okay, so it's meant for me," I answered. "Does it say there how to open it? Can you decipher that part?"

"This wasn't given to me," he said, returning the box. "It's quite possible this box is meant to be opened only by you."

"I'm not a mage," I said. "I don't know how to deal with these kinds of artifacts, except to put them in a pocket or on a shelf somewhere."

"When keepsakers were first created, they were unique to the person receiving them," Monty said. "I'm sure the method of accessing this one will come to you at some point. In the meantime—"

"The test?"

"Indeed," Monty said, looking around. "I will have to thank Calisto for providing us with this space."

We stood in an empty room. Every surface held intricate shimmering designs etched into the stone. The entrance, which was also the exit to the room, was sealed off with a section of vibrating blue energy.

"Why couldn't this place be built back home?" I asked, looking at the designs. "Not that I'm some expert in runic design."

"The closest anyone has ever come to building a sequence room on this scale is the 'migraine room' you experienced at Fordey. Even then, that room needed a catalyst."

I shuddered at the memory of visiting the migraine room.

"This place doesn't have a Black Heart though," I said, looking around. "And I don't have a migraine trying to liquefy my brain."

"It doesn't need one. Look at the designs again."

I stepped over to one of the many designs and examined it closely. Inside the groove, I saw small crystals which gave them their shimmering effect.

"Are these crystals—?"

"They would be the equivalent of the Black Heart ground to dust and then spread throughout this room."

"This room is easily ten times larger than the one in Fordey," I said. "That would make the center gem—"

"Roughly ten feet across," Monty said. "If it were concentrated in that form, it would be lethal. Like this,"—

he waved an arm around the room—"it maintains its power without overloading the subject."

"The subject. Which would be me in this case."

"Precisely," Monty said, pointing to the floor. "Please stand in this circle. Whatever you do, do not leave the circle."

I put the keepsaker back in a pocket, and stood in the circle he indicated in the center of the floor. It was a slightly raised area, roughly four feet in diameter, covered in seven concentric circles, and interlaced with more runic designs.

"Fine, let's get it over with," I said. "Where's Peaches?"

"You won't need your creature for this," Monty said, touching parts of the circle around my feet. "You aren't in imminent risk, at least not to my knowledge."

"I call excruciating pain a high-risk situation."

"It can't be helped. Besides he's currently indisposed."

"He's stuffing his face somewhere, isn't he?"

"Kitchen," Monty said, somewhat distracted as he paced the circle. "Calisto is providing him and her mammoth bear with food."

"Of course, the traitor would leave me for meat. He has a one-track stomach."

"He doesn't need to be here and it's best if he isn't. Your creature may think you're in danger and try to save you."

"Can't have that happening. Depriving me of the agony would be unacceptable."

"Indeed," Monty said with a nod. "It would also take time. Priming this room is a complicated process. One I don't wish to repeat."

"Is it still night, or have three weeks passed?" I asked. "Time is crazy in this place."

"Only for us," Monty said. "Since we are not native to this plane, I do think that time flows differently here for us. The sooner we conduct the test, the better."

"For you."

"Stop pouting," Monty answered, standing in the middle of the room. "This will only be excruciating for a few moments...I think."

"Your certainty instills me with so much confidence. I'm just brimming with anticipation at how fun this will be."

"There are variables," Monty said, motioning for me to stand in the center. "Chief among them, your curse and being a non-mage."

"When you went through this," I said, moving to stand over the specific runes he pointed out, "how bad was it?"

"It was...unpleasant," he said after a pause. "At least what I could remember."

"How long will this thing take?" I asked. "I may have other things on my schedule today."

"Such as?"

"I was thinking of having a no anesthesia root canal followed by having my fingernails removed with some pliers," I deadpanned. "Nothing major, just a splash of evening torture to cap things off."

"I'll make sure to clear the schedule, then," he answered. "You may also want to look into that dental trauma."

"I don't have dental trauma, I just dislike dentists with a passion," I said. "So do my teeth. It's a mild case of PTSD."

"Since when have you had post-traumatic stress disorder?"

"Post Traumatic Stress of Dentistry...not as bad, but I feel scarred or something."

He reached into a pocket, pulled out a small case, and handed it to me.

"Or something, indeed," Monty said. "You'll need this. Put it in before the third ring is filled, or your dental nightmares will become a reality as you grind your teeth to dust."

I took the small case and opened it. Inside, was a mouthpiece, similar to those worn by boxers when they fought. This one appeared to be industrial strength, and was designed to cover both upper and lower sets of teeth.

"Really, Monty," I said, closing the case. "You shouldn't have. Does this mean we're going steady?"

"If by steady, you mean the steady decline of your mental capacities, then yes."

"How long?" I asked. "Seriously."

"Not long," he answered, heading to the door. "Remember to stay in the circle, or we have to reset and do it again."

"I won't be leaving the circle," I said. "We aren't doing this again."

"Hopefully we'll have some conclusive results...if you survive the process."

I stared at him.

"Get out."

TEN

Monty headed to the doorway, pressed his hand on the wall next to the door, and stepped through the blue energy field.

"For the record," I said, "the fact that you're out there while this test is going on doesn't make me feel any better."

"I know," Monty said. "The energies released during this process are volatile. Remember when I said we all vibrate at a specific frequency?"

"Vaguely. I start tuning you out when you get Zillerfied."

"Well, my presence in there with you would negate the test and possibly put us all at great risk," Monty answered as he gestured. "The outcome could damage the Keep, something I'm sure you're averse to being a part of."

"Extremely averse," I said. "Calisto looks dangerous. Let's not piss her off, thanks."

"Very well," he said. "Are you ready?"

"To go through an unknown amount of excruciating pain for an unspecified period of time?"

"Yes."

"Do I look ready to you?" I asked. "Just begin."

He gestured one more time. I made sure I was standing inside the circle. The blue section of energy grew opaque. I could still make out his silhouette, and saw him raise an arm. The next moment, he slammed a hand into the wall of energy and yelled something unintelligible.

For a few seconds, nothing happened. I was about to tell him that his test was broken, when the runic designs etched into the walls blazed with blue energy. The room thrummed with power as the energy flowed down the walls and into the floor.

I stood on the circle, a cold sweat covering my brow as I noticed the energy creeping closer to where I stood. It was the same feeling of dread as hearing the whirr of the dentist drill as it slowly approached. Clearly, I had a dental trauma.

The temperature of the room dropped. After a few seconds, I could see my exhalations as it entered Arctic meat locker conditions. The outer ring of the circle filled with energy, and a jolt ran through my body. It started off subtly, then ratcheted up to extreme pins and needles, moments later.

"This...is not fun!" I yelled, as the current of energy ran through my legs. "Definitely not...fun!"

"Conserve your energy, Simon," Monty called out. "Each ring that fills will increase the discomfort. You may want to focus on remaining within the circle."

I tried to move my legs and realized they were rooted to the center of the circle.

"Like I'm going anywhere," I muttered. "I'm stuck in this circle."

"That means it's working. Not much longer now."

"We are going to need to discuss time frames when this is over," I said. "I think we have a different understanding of...AHH!"

"That would be the second ring," Monty said calmly. "I'd refrain from speech at this point. Please insert the mouthpiece."

I wanted to answer, but my jaw started to clench. I quickly put in the mouthpiece as the energy in my body increased. So far, everything above my waist was still mobile, barely, but I could feel the energy creeping up my spine. It started with a jab in my lower back, which quickly became a muscle spasm, followed by a searing sensation barbecuing my midsection.

"Oh....shit," I mumbled through gritted teeth. "This is going to be bad."

The third circle filled with energy.

A spike of ice drove itself through the top of my head and into my brain, giving me the worst case of brain freeze in recorded history. The energy that was slowly creeping, stood and sprinted up my spine, slamming me in the base of my neck to meet the ice spike drilling down.

A migraine of epic proportions spread through my skull, partially blinding me. At this point, all I could do was groan in pain as I noticed the fourth circle slowly filling with energy. Tears streamed down my cheeks and ears.

Something was wrong. Even through the haze of pain, I had the strangest thought. *Since when did I start crying from my ears?* I struggled to raise my hand to the side of my head. It came away bloody.

That can't be good.

The fourth circle filled and I lost all sight to the pain. It gripped my body and squeezed, a vise of agony and delirium. For a moment, the pain overwhelmed me and I blacked out.

"Hello, Splinter," a familiar voice whispered. "This looks invigorating."

"Ka...Karma?"

"It's been a while."

"Before you get slaphappy, I didn't press my mark."

"I know," she said. "It's possible you're imagining this. Your grip on reality seems to be tenuous these days."

"My grip is just fine, it's reality that's acting shaky."

"Probably more than usual, lately."

"Wouldn't even know where to begin," I said. "How are you even here?"

"Where you go...I go."

"Now you sound like Peaches," I replied. "Why can't I see you?"

"Right now, you can't see...in more ways than one."

"Am I hallucinating?" I asked, confused. "What's happening?"

"It's all a riddle, wrapped in a mystery, inside an enigma," she said. "By the way, is the mage *trying* to kill you?"

"I don't think so," I said. "He's trying to figure out what's wrong with me."

"Plenty, but this method looks particularly lethal," she answered, "even for the "Chosen of Kali'. Tell me, Splinter"—I could feel her breath on my neck—"do you know the difference between Karma and Fate?"

It took a moment to gather my thoughts through the haze of pain.

"Karma is the result of what I do, my actions," I said, wondering where she was going with this question. "Fate means that things are predestined, I don't have a choice."

"Good," she said. "Remember that, you're going to need it soon."

A bone-jarring slap rocked my jaw, and removed all doubt of hallucination. I was back in my body, doing the torture tango. The pain from her violent caress was manageable compared to what I had just experienced prior to her visit. Nothing like a wake up slap from the personification of causality to put things in perspective.

I looked down and saw the last ring was filling with blue energy. I must have been out for rings five and six. The pain had reached such a level that my body was blazing, trying to heal me. The seventh, innermost ring filled and a column of blue energy blasted into my body, blinding me again.

That's when I screamed.

ELEVEN

Pain has a way of bringing clarity.

Normally, we as humans dislike pain, but it's a sensation like any other. Feeling cold, or hot, or pain was just the way our brains dealt with the sensory stimuli of being in the world.

The pain I experienced when the seventh circle filled with energy changed my mind of that theory. That indescribable moment of agony, although brief, imprinted itself into every cell of my body.

I sat next to the now dormant circle as the room slowly spun around me. The pain, like most pain, was beginning to fade. The memory of the agony lingered, but the visceral sensation had dulled. My body flushed hot, dealing with the damage, but something felt off.

I looked up into Calisto's face as she bandaged my arms. Behind her stood a concerned-looking Monty. Next to him sat a worried Peaches. I knew he was worried from the tone of his rumble.

<I'll be fine, boy.>

<You don't look fine. You didn't sound fine when you yelled for me.>

<I don't remember yelling for you.>

<Which means you are not fine. Why is the nice bear lady putting cloth on your arms?>

<I don't know. My body usually heals on its own.>

<If you need help, I could lick you. My saliva can heal you.>

<Thanks, boy. I think she has it handled. Let's save the slobber therapy for when I'm really hurt.>

<You should ask her for meat. The bear lady has good meat.>

<I'm not hungry, thanks. I am sore, though.>

<If you ate meat, you wouldn't be sore or smell like fire.>

<The energy circle tried to cook me. It was too much power.>

<Not for me. I moved you. Because I eat meat.>

<Of course. I'm sure it has nothing to do with your being a super indestructible hellhound. Just your diet.>

"You three need to leave this plane as soon as possible," Calisto said, wrapping my arms. "This plane is becoming lethally dangerous for you."

"Why are you wrapping my arms?" I asked. "My body usually—"

"It's repairing itself, Simon, but the damage is extensive," Monty said, stepping forward. "It's recovering too slowly."

"Too slowly?" I asked. "That seventh ring was beyond agony. I'm surprised I'm even here at all."

"Very few survive the seventh ring of a phasic scan."

"You do that to all the shifting mages?"

"Yes," Monty answered. "The seventh ring is usually reserved for the higher levels."

"Excuse me? What do you mean, reserved for higher levels? Higher levels of what?"

"The phasic scan runs according to the level of the mage in the circle," Monty explained. "In your case, being a non-mage, I estimated a max level of three rings. I didn't anticipate it even being able to go to the last ring, let alone it actually doing it."

"Damn thing fried me crispy,"—I looked down at my burned arms—"judging from the insta-tan."

"You should be dead," Calisto added. "Seventh ring scans"—she glanced at Monty—"require the presence of at least one Archmage if not two. This was reckless and foolish."

"How did you guess our nicknames?" I asked with a grin. "I'm foolish, he's reckless."

"I'm serious," Calisto answered. "You've been here too long."

"We get that often. Mostly after Monty blows up something. Usually a building or two."

"Going to a seventh ring nearly blew apart the Keep," she answered. "If your hellhound hadn't rushed here, it would have been too late. We would have been sweeping up your remains."

I glanced down at Peaches. I must've called him when the seventh ring hit, even though I had no recollection of calling for him.

"The test?" I asked. "Did it work?"

Monty glanced at Calisto.

"Tell him," she said. "He should know."

"I should know what?" I asked, looking at Monty. "Tell me."

"The test worked...somewhat," Monty said, hesitatingly. "The results were hard to decipher. Seeing as how all of the rings were activated."

"Somewhat? What do you mean, somewhat? What was hard to decipher? Because the pain I went through was easy to understand."

"You aren't poisoned."

"That's good news," I said, feeling the weight lift off my shoulders. Then I noticed their expressions. "That *is* good news...right?"

"It's not that simple," Monty said. "You aren't poisoned, but you're affecting reality around you."

"I do have a tendency to make an impact, but I'm guessing from the look on your faces, that's not what you mean."

They both shook their heads slowly.

"I've never seen anything like it. At least, not on a human," Calisto said. "Whatever is acting as the catalyst has enormous power. Even to the degree that it's affecting you here, on this plane."

"Never seen anything like what?"

"You're affecting causality," Calisto answered. "The only other person I've seen with that ability was Emiko, the first Jade Demon, and she's dead."

"That sounds encouraging," I said. "What do you mean, affecting causality?"

"This could bring us, specifically you, unwanted attention," Monty said. "The kind that would think nothing of erasing you."

"Erasing me?" I asked. "What are you talking about?"

"There are beings tasked with keeping order," Monty answered. "If you are upsetting the balance of causality, they will want to restore that balance."

"Restore the balance?"

"Yes, that is their purpose. Fortunately, we have avoided their attention...until now."

"You mean, eliminating me?" I asked. "They're going to have a hard time pulling that one off."

"It means *erasing* you and any trace of your existence," Monty said. "You cease to exist, past, present, and future."

"It means you need to leave this plane...now," Calisto answered. "I'm sorry, but your presence here is affecting the integrity of the wards around the Keep. If the wards fail—"

"We understand," Monty said. "Thank you for allowing us to use the Keep."

"Glad one of us understands," I said. "Thank you for feeding Peaches."

"He's a good hellhound," Calisto said, glancing down at Peaches. "He probably saved your life today."

"Not the first time."

"I doubt it will be the last," Calisto said. "Feel free to visit if you ever get your situation resolved. Give my regards to your uncle. Until then, kindly stay on your plane."

It was one of the most polite 'get out of my plane and don't come back' comments we'd gotten. Usually when we were asked to leave a place, explosions and angry words were part of the request, along with threats of extreme pain. This was a nice non-violent change.

Monty gestured and formed a portal.

"Thank you again," Monty said. "I will pass on your words to my uncle. I'm sure he would be interested in your assistance at the Golden Circle."

"Inform him that a visit is not needed. We are still dealing with the fallout from the last time he stayed here."

Monty raised an eyebrow.

"I didn't know he had been here," Monty said. "Was this a recent visit?"

"Recent enough that most of the Unholy want him dead, except maybe the Dreadwolves," Calisto answered, with nod. "They probably want to chew on him for a bit, first."

"Sounds like my uncle," Monty replied. "I'll inform him a visit is not preferred."

"Tell him I'll reach out for the locations and get back to him."

Monty nodded and looked at me.

"Thank you again," I said. "If you ever need help, you know where to find us."

"Thank you for the kind offer," Calisto said, "but if I ever come to you for help, you can rest assured the situation will be beyond apocalyptic."

"In that case," I said, "hope to never see you?"

"Exactly," Calisto answered. "Goodbye, Simon."

I motioned to Peaches and we stepped through the portal.

The light from the afternoon sun crept across the floor when we arrived on the other side of the portal in front of Dex's door. The runes on the door were still pulsing as I examined them.

"These runes are still blinking in and out."

"I'm aware," Monty said, moving to the conference room as I headed to the kitchen. "We need to determine how much time has passed."

"We were at the Keep for a day," I said. "At least according to the wacky time over there."

"Simon?" Monty called out. "You need to come to the conference room."

"I'm hungry," I said, sounding like my hellhound. "Give me a minute."

"I'm afraid this can't wait. You need to see this...now."

I headed to the conference room, wondering what could be so urgent.

"I didn't scratch the conference table," I called out. "Neither did Peaches."

<Did you scratch the big table in the conference room?>

<With my teeth or my paws?>

<The correct answer is, none of the above.>

<Oh, then none of the above. Can I have some meat?>

<Not if you scratched the table. You know how Monty gets.>

<You called him crumpy. Is that good?>

<He's cranky and grumpy. Crumpy is just easier.>

<Should I call him the crumpy man?>

<Not really. He doesn't like to be called cranky or grumpy. I doubt he'll prefer crumpy.>

"This is not about some scratches," Monty replied. "This has to do with your attracting attention."

"I told you, I'm low-key," I said. "I don't do the attracting. You and my hellhound do all of the attracting."

"Not this time," he said. "You have a guest."

"A guest?" I asked. "I don't do guests. How did this guest even get past the security?"

"I'm sure she didn't encounter any difficulty circumventing our defenses."

"She?" I asked. "I thought Chi was MIA?"

"This is decidedly not your vampire."

The only person who fit the description of unannounced visits was Michiko. Only Peaches seemed to deter her surprise visits.

"Well then," I said as I approached. "How do you know our guest is here for me?"

"Call it intuition."

"Fine, I'll be right there," I called back. "Did you install corridors of chaos without telling me?"

"Now, Simon."

The urgency in his voice concerned me. Whoever was in the conference room had Monty on edge. I've seen him drink tea in the middle of pitched battles with some of the nastiest creatures on the planet. Monty didn't get on edge unless the threat was serious.

If Monty was nervous, there was a good chance that who or whatever was waiting for me was a threat. I looked down at my hellhound padding silently next to me.

<*We may have to deal with some trouble, boy.*>

<*Trouble?*> He sniffed the air. <*I don't smell anything bad... except you.*>

<*Someone is waiting for me. Just be ready.*>

<*Do you think they have meat?*>

<*Somehow I really doubt they came here to bring me meat.*>

<*You need better friends. Good friends would bring you meat.*>

<*I don't have meat friends. My friends are usually destroying things around me.*>

<*You need better friends.*>

<*Mine are great, they just don't gift me with meat because of you.*>

<*They should.*>

<*I'll make sure to have some words with them. In the meantime, keep on your toes.*>

<*I don't walk well on my toes.*>

<Figure of speech. Get ready to unleash your Barkour skills in case we have to fight.>

<What is barkour? Is that when I speak?>

<And blink in-between and all over the place, scaring people. Barkour.>

<I like Barkour. I will be ready.>

I rounded the corner and headed down the small hallway that led to the conference room. I swore that on some days, our offices felt larger than usual inside. It wouldn't surprise me, considering Dex had a room in our space. It would be just like him to inscribe expansion runes all over the property.

I entered the conference room, and sitting at the far end was a woman.

"Hello, Simon," she said. "We need to talk about your current level of impact."

Monty stood by the doorway looking upset, which is saying plenty, considering he always looked upset. Something about this woman set him off. Starting with the fact that she bypassed all of our security and was sitting in our conference room, thumbing through a book. I couldn't sense her energy signature, which raised all kinds of red flags. The air around her shimmered, giving that side of the conference table a subtle mirage effect.

Usually when someone or something came across as an empty void, we were facing power several orders of magnitude beyond what we could deal with. This presence, and its lack of signature, was up there with Hades-level capability.

"Are you sure she isn't here for you?" I asked, glancing at Monty. "She definitely seems like one of those magey types. Do you see how she's dressed?"

Monty shook his head.

"I'm certain. I don't make a habit of seeking audiences with powerful beings," Monty said. "That's your department."

"I'm not doing it on purpose, you know," I said. "They look for me."

"Of course they do," Monty motioned to the woman with his head. "Don't be rude."

I turned to face the end of the conference table.

"You seem to know who I am," I said, opening my jacket and making sure Grim Whisper was accessible. "Who are you?"

"I'm Fate."

TWELVE

She slowly closed the book, gave me a small smile and focused on me.

Now I was really nervous.

Appearing in our conference room without setting off our security was bad, but I knew that smile. It was the kind of smile that said 'I'm about to make your life a living hell, and enjoy myself while I do so'.

"Fate?" I said, cautiously. "I thought there were three of you?"

"There are," the woman said. "Clotho, Lachesis, and Atropos"—she held up a finger for each name—"we three are one. We are Fate."

I looked around the conference room, even crouching down to look under the conference table.

"I'm not seeing anyone else," I said, peeking over the edge of the table as Peaches settled into his spot underneath it. "Did you lose the other two?"

"Simon..." Monty said, shaking his head. "She is in a triune form."

"Like I'm supposed to know that? How exactly am I supposed to know she's walking around like a 'buy one, get three special'?"

"It's obvious, if you look."

"I am looking," I said, pointing two fingers to my eyes and then turning the fingers to Fate. "One person, not three. Are you sure she's not some renegade mage on Golden Circle business?"

I examined Fate, and saw just the one figure sitting in the chair. Nothing about her told me she was a triune being. The Morrigan, on the other hand, definitely gave off the 'I'm much more than I appear' vibe.

Fate was dressed in typical mage attire. Black Armani power suit, white shirt with a silver pocket kerchief. A silver triquetra pin rested in her short black hair. She leaned forward and peered at me over silver-rimmed glasses.

She was obviously masking her energy signature, I had just never encountered someone who could do it so completely. I still leaned toward overpowered mage. The only thing that threw me, not that I was an expert on mages, was that she read like 'more than human', somehow, and yet was completely not there.

If I didn't see her in front of me, she would be invisible to my senses. The one thing that stood out was her iridescent eyes. The afternoon light that entered the conference room made her eyes subtly rainbow-like when she moved her head.

"You're looking, but not seeing," Monty replied, but remained standing. "It is obvious if you knew *how* to look."

"Not obvious at all," I said. "Only seeing one person here. Are the other two invisible? Hiding maybe?"

"She is trisected, like the Morrigan," Monty said. "One being, three parts."

"The Morrigan I get," I said with a shudder. "I still remember the bad catheter at your ass-kicking with TK."

"Reckoning, and its Badb Catha. It seems this being is similar."

"I thought the Fates were supposed to be old hags over a cauldron," I said, looking at the woman. "I'm not getting the crone vibe here."

"Our mythos has been twisted many times over millennia," Fate said. "Please sit, Simon."

"Have we met?" I asked, taking a chair at the opposite end of the table. "Did Monty tell you my—"

"I know all names," she said. "I'm Fa—"

"Yes, I get that, you're Fate and all that," I said. "Why are you here?"

"We need to talk."

"I don't have anything to say."

"That would be a first," Monty said, sitting to my right. "This goes back to what I said earlier about your level of attraction."

"I could stand to be a little less attractive right now," I said. "Why can't I attract low-level beings, like Caffeina, goddess of javambrosia. She could threaten me with a mug of delicious coffee. I'd even settle for Hops, the demigod of beer drinking and carousing?"

"I don't think either of those exist," Monty said.

"O, ye of little faith," I said. "We just need to believe."

"I *believe* those are made up figments of your imagination," Monty said, and then turned to look at Fate. "Why are you here?"

"You know why, mage. The same reason you spent

three days finding out what you knew to be true from the onset."

"Three days?" I asked. "What do you mean, three days?"

"You have been absent from this plane for three days," Fate said. "Discovering the obvious."

"She is definitely sounding like your crowd, clear as dirt," I said, glancing at Monty. "Can you elaborate?"

"We experienced time dilation and constriction simultaneously," Monty answered, still looking at Fate. "Time flowed faster here than at the Keep."

"I got that part," I said. "The other part, the 'what you knew to be true from the onset' part. Can you explain that?"

"Do you recall when I mentioned those beings that would think nothing of erasing you?"

"Vividly," I said. "Is that what this is? A disintegration?"

"You are impacting reality," Monty said. "Hence our guest."

"No shit," I snapped. "I impact reality every day. It's what I—what we—do. Since when does that concern Fate?"

"My working theory is that it's having negative effects."

"It is," Fate said. "Tell me, Simon, do you know what fate is?"

This brought back Karma's question to me while I had been in the midst of the torture test.

"I can tell you what I understand fate to be," I said. "A scary looking being currently sitting in my conference room. How's that?"

"Fate is that which is destined to be," Fate said. "You

have violated the laws of causality, and balance must be restored."

"What? I've done no such thing," I said, confused. "I don't recall violating any laws of anything, but if you insist, just write me a ticket and I'll take care of it."

"You mask your fear with humor," Fate answered. "Has anyone told you how irritating that can be?"

"Repeatedly," I said, glancing at Monty. "Write your ticket, I'll pay your fate fine and we can a call it a day."

"Who are we speaking with?" Monty asked. "Which of the three are you?"

"It's Fate, Monty," I said. "She already said who she was."

"I am Lachesis the Alloter, and you, Simon Strong, have been a royal pain in my ass."

"I don't even know you," I said. "I usually know who I'm aggravating. You, I don't know."

"You weren't born immortal," Lachesis said. "Once you became one, your transition disrupted everything."

"Hey," I said, suddenly offended, "it's not like I woke up one day and said: 'You know what? Today I'm going to become immortal'. If you have an issue with my immortality, take it up with Kali."

"I don't have to," Lachesis said. "I'm here to offer you a choice, Chosen of Kali."

"A choice? What choice?"

"Restore balance or be erased."

THIRTEEN

"Restore balance or be erased?" I asked. "How exactly am I supposed to restore balance?"

"I think she means lose your immortality," Monty said. "Become mortal again."

"Is Monty right?" I asked. "You want me to become mortal again?"

"This is not about what I *want*," Fate said. "This is about what *must* be done, to restore balance."

"So you're saying my being immortal, something that was done *to* me, mind you, is jeopardizing all of reality?"

"You were not born this way," Fate answered slowly. "Becoming immortal has allowed you to interact with beings and situations you never would have impacted had you been mortal."

"Am I supposed to just go up to Kali and say: 'I need you to remove the curse', and that's supposed to work?" I asked. "Have you ever met Kali? She doesn't seem like the kind to take requests, least of all mine. She *cursed* me. It wasn't a gift."

"Why aren't we speaking to Atropos?" Monty asked. "Why you?"

"You want more of them to appear, really?" I asked. "I'm good with one of the three."

"The Alloter measures the thread, but Atropos is the one who cuts it," Monty continued, looking at Fate. "Why are we having this discussion with you? Wouldn't Atropos be the one to present Simon with this choice? Unless..."

"Unless they can't take direct action against me," I said, having a sudden realization. "Unless...I'm mortal."

"Your thread cannot be cut in its current state," Fate said. "This is true."

"Seems like there's more," I said. "What aren't you saying?"

"The balance must be restored. We cannot sever your thread currently, but the threads of those your life touches"—she glanced at Monty—"can be."

"Is that a threat?" I asked. "Are you threatening those close to me?"

"I am Fate. I have no need for empty threats. I will tell you what will occur if you continue along this path," she answered, as her voice transformed, increasing in volume and tone. It suddenly sounded like more than one person was speaking at once. "You will heed my decree."

"I'm heeding," I said, rubbing a temple "but you need to lower the volume. I've had one hell of a headache, very little coffee, and your volume isn't helping. Dial it down."

She stared at me for a few seconds, nodded her head and smiled.

"You will either restore the balance and your mortality," she said, lowering her blended voice, "or everyone you have impacted will have their threads severed."

"Sounds like a threat to me," I said. "What happened to not making threats?"

"I said I have no need for *empty* threats."

"Ah, yours are *full* of menace then," I answered. "Since when does Fate get involved in day to day affairs? I thought you three were big picture, cataclysmic overseers, that sort of stuff."

"My very existence defines day-to-day *and* the 'big picture' as you call it," she said. "Your immortal presence in the day-to-day affects the larger scheme of things."

"Yet you threaten those close to me."

"You think you are alone and have few people in your life, don't you?" Fate asked. "You pretend that you are isolated, now that you are immortal."

"I'm not exactly a social butterfly," I said. "Monty, Peaches, Michiko and a few others are my circle. Don't need much more. My life is complicated as is. I'd say that's isolated. My circle is small."

"Wrong," Fate answered. "This entire city"—she waved an arm around—"has been set on a different path because of *your* actions. Even now, the repercussions of your influence are impacting others."

I laughed, but then grew serious when I realized she wasn't joking.

"You're serious?" I asked in disbelief. "My actions? What are you talking about?"

"*That* is why we are speaking to you," Monty said, understanding while I was still in the dark. "We altered their timelines."

"Glad *you* know why. Care to share?"

"Every time we saved the city or averted a disaster, we

changed the fate of the city and the people in it," Monty said. "We altered lives and outcomes."

"You have created a raveled mess, Simon Strong," Fate said, crossing her arms. "Your participation in the events of this city have rippled across countless lives."

"We *saved* lives," I said. "What were we supposed to do? Sit back and watch it happen?"

"You weren't supposed to be involved at all," Fate answered. "*You* upset the balance."

"What about Monty?" I asked. "Why are you making this all about me? No offense, Monty."

"None taken, I'm curious as well," Monty answered. "Simon didn't act on his own. Why single him out?"

"His involvement set you on a different path," Fate answered. "He is the catalyst, the nexus of the disruption. If he had remained mortal after your first case, you would have left this city. You can extrapolate the rest."

"You say that like I had a choice," I snapped. "Kali cursed me. I didn't ask for this."

"You chose to act of your own free will," Fate said, her voice grim. "No one forced you to make the choices you made. That was all you, not Kali nor anyone else...just you."

She was right. Didn't mean I had to like it.

"What? I should've retreated to some mountaintop and sat crossed-legged until Kali changed her mind?"

"You should have done everything possible to reverse your immortality," she said, "because you knew it was not the natural order of your life. You chose to exploit it."

"You make it seem like I wanted to be immortal," I said. "I was working a case and got in between two gods who were pissed at each other."

"Seems like you make a habit of being in the wrong place at the wrong time."

"It's a gift," I said. "Kali cursed me alive because she wanted me to suffer. I'm not exploiting it, but I'm also not going out of my way to have a conversation with a goddess of destruction either."

"That is not my concern," Fate replied, standing. "It is a matter you need to resolve with her. She will either agree, and you can continue to live out the remaining days of a mortal life, or she will refuse, and we will have to take...steps. To restore the balance."

Another threat. This one sounded worse than the first one. It was probably the way she paused before the word 'steps' that set off my warning system.

"Steps?" I asked, concerned. "What steps?"

"While it's true your thread can't be cut now, it was not always this way," Fate replied. "If you cannot alter your immortality, we will be forced to go back and sever it when you were mortal, before you—"

"Upset the balance, I get it," I finished, looking at Monty. "Can they do that? Go back to a time in my life when I was mortal and"—I made a scissor motion with my fingers—"snip?"

"I don't know," Monty said, pensively. "I've never heard of a retroactive timeline correction. This is highly irregular and unprecedented."

"'Highly irregular and unprecedented' sums up my life in one sentence."

"We can and will take the appropriate action to restore equilibrium," Fate said. "If you don't or can't resolve this, we will. No one escapes or alters their fate. No one."

"You want me to find Kali and convince her she made a

mistake," I said, exasperated. "Clearly, you haven't dealt with gods. Admitting mistakes isn't in their vocabulary. I wouldn't even know where to start."

"Start there," she said, pointing to the mark on my hand. "That is more than just a symbol. It is a key...use it."

"A key?" I said, looking down at my hand. "What are you talking about?"

"You have seven days," Fate answered, picking up her book from the conference table. "That is all the time I can allot. If you are not mortal by that time, you will face a simple choice. Have your thread severed, or allow those whose your life touched, to perish."

"I just want to say that, as choices go, that one sucks and is far from simple."

"Life is rarely simple and yours is more complex than most."

"What did you mean by repercussions? What repercussions?"

"You will realize that everything is connected," Fate answered, making it clear she held a black belt in cryptic speech. "Those close to you will be affected first, along with the places of power in this city."

"Well that clears it all up," I said, frustrated. "You do realize this entire city is practically a place of power?"

"Don't be naive, Simon," she replied. "Narrow your focus where the two intersect and you will begin to see the effects of your current state."

"What? I don't even understand—"

"Seven days, Simon. Goodbye."

She vanished. A second later, a large hourglass materialized on the conference table. The silver sand slowly fell into the bottom bulb.

"I guess it could be worse," I said, moving closer to the hourglass. "She could have gone modern with one of those digital countdown timers."

"This is serious, Simon," Monty said. "We need help on this."

"I agree," I said. "Who do you think we should get? Because I'm fresh out of ideas on how to deal with Fate before she gets all snippy."

"That would be Atropos and her shears," Monty said. "Although it seems all three were speaking at the end. Still, the energy signature felt familiar somehow."

"Familiar how?" I asked. "You know who she is?"

"It's impossible," Monty said, waving my words away. "I must be mistaken."

"Fine. How do we stop Atrophy from cutting my string?"

"Atropos, and it's your thread, not string."

"Thread, string. *Tomayto, tomahto,*" I said. "How do we stop her?"

"I've never faced a personification of Fate," Monty said. "Is she like Karma?"

"Nothing and no one is like Karma, trust me."

"We need an expert on life and death," Monty said. "Someone who could at least point us in the right direction."

"Right direction?" I said, raising my voice. "Were you not paying attention? That was Fate! She gave me a week, and you want to go in the right direction?"

"I was paying attention, but were you?"

"Of course I was," I said. "I especially heard the part about either severing my string or the erasing everyone I've impacted."

"Not that," Monty said, waving my words away. "The other part."

"Giving me a week to find and convince Kali, the goddess of destruction, to remove her curse and make me mortal?"

"The other, other part."

"Now you sound as clear as Fate. Elaborate please."

"You will impact others close to you and places of power," Monty said. "Like you said, this entire city appears to be a hub of power. If that hub is compromised and the balance broken, your curse would be the least of our worries."

"How am I supposed to find Kali? As destructive as you are, it doesn't make me friendly with a goddess of destruction."

"Kali is also known as a goddess of creation, among other things," Monty said, "which is probably how she managed to curse you alive."

"You know, I wasn't really paying attention to the creation side of things when she cursed me," I said. "She seemed pretty pissed we interfered in her 500 year op to stop Shiva. It slipped my mind to ask if she was going to demonstrate her creative abilities."

"There are several important things we are missing," Monty said. "Why did Kali curse only you? I was there with you."

"Good question," I said. "When we find her, why don't you ask her?"

"More importantly, Fate said something relevant."

"The whole 'ending me or those close to me' comment really focused my attention. I must've missed the other relevant part. Enlighten me."

"She said no one escapes or alters their fate, no one."

"I remember that, so?"

"It's not true," Monty said. "I personally know several people who have altered their fate through their actions and will. Myself included."

"Are you saying Fate is lying?"

"I think she is presenting the truth in a manner that benefits her," Monty said after a pause. "It would be like my saying your creature is a dog. Technically true, he appears to belong to the canine species, but it is far from the complete truth."

"That's just typical. Every time we deal with beings of power, they seem to have some sort of hidden agenda," I said. "Specifically gods and their power plays."

"True," Monty said with a nod. "It may be their reality differs from our own, due to their natural state of being. Gods operate on a timetable of millennia. Humans,"—he glanced at me—"at least most humans, must seem insignificant in terms of scale, their lives being mere moments in the grander scheme of things."

"Just because we don't live as long doesn't mean we should be made pawns in their games," I said, angry. "They always think we're just specks of dust to be brushed away when we irritate them."

"Apparently, Fate would like to revert you back to dust status," Monty said. "It would seem you have become more than just an irritant. There is more going on here, but I'm not seeing it."

"Will this expert you mentioned be able to see it?" I asked.

"I believe so."

“Who exactly is this expert on life and death you’re referring to?”

“I’d say it’s past time to get your creature some quality meat,” Monty said, standing to leave the room. “I think pastrami is his protein of choice?”

“I think the Randy Rump is still closed I think. Besides, Jim would prefer we called first before popping by. He mentioned something about activating the extra security the last time I spoke to him.”

“I was thinking a little older and less alive.”

“Oh, *that* expert.”

<*Come on, boy. We’re going to the place.*>

<*Yes! I’m starving.*>

FOURTEEN

I opened the rear door to the Dark Goat and let Peaches, the sprawlmaster, climb in. The suspension creaked and the car listed slightly to one side, as my hellhound adjusted to the backseat and took up all of the room.

I shook my head in amazement, sliding in behind the wheel, and shaking off what I called the DG skin crawl. Peaches was going to be too large for the Dark Goat soon.

"I need a moment to recalibrate some of these runes," Monty said as he touched some of the symbols on the dashboard. "Olga informed me one of the new attendants tried to move the vehicle a few days ago. He's still in intensive care."

"She didn't tell them?" I asked, surprised. "I spoke to her."

"Every attendant knows to leave this vehicle alone," Monty said, gesturing as violet symbols floated from his fingers and landed on the dashboard. "The one in question chose not to, opting to drive it into a parking space."

"Sounds like some kind of prank. Maybe you should have a word with the attendants?"

"I shall. The last thing we need is a vehicular casualty due to immature behavior," Monty said. "It appears this young man didn't believe the warnings."

"I'm sure he's believing now," I said. "Is he going to be okay?"

"Olga tells me he went prematurely gray. He was removed from the vehicle in a near catatonic state, babbling something about demons. Other than that, he should be fine."

I stared at the gesturing Monty for a few seconds.

"Sounds like he got lucky," I said after a few moments. "DG almost toasted him."

"Indeed. Are you certain you want to name it the 'Dark Goat'? It sounds ominous."

"Because it is," I said. "People get creeped out just walking by it, forget about driving it. I get the skin crawl every time and I'm cursed. Don't you feel off, getting in the Dark Goat?"

"Are you wondering if I 'get off' riding in a potential death machine?"

"When you put it like that it sounds dirty," I said. "You know what I mean. Don't your mage super powers pick up on the energy signals it gives off?"

"I'm aware of its...properties," Monty answered, still dealing with the dash. "I've felt worse. I do know better than to try and drive this vehicle though. I'm a mage, not insane."

"I thought those two words explained the same condition?"

"In some cases, yes. Not in mine."

"Not yet?"

"Not ever," Monty affirmed. "I'm in full possession of my faculties and intend to remain that way."

"Usually when someone has to explain they are in full possession of their faculties...they aren't."

"I didn't know you also dabbled in psychology," Monty said with a glance. "Where did you study?"

"You may have heard of it...UMAD? The University of Mages Are Deranged? I've had plenty of real world experience ever since I started there. Very exclusive. Beyond Ivy League."

"I'm certain it's beyond. Just like the name of this car."

"I think the Dark Goat sounds perfect. Driver's choice."

He waved my words away as he kept calibrating the symbols.

<Can I have extra meat because I smelled you?>

<I'll ask Ezra to give you some healthy pastrami. You really need to be on a low-fat meat diet. If you keep eating like this, you're going to break the Dark Goat. Did you see how it tilted when you got in?>

<A low-fat diet sounds like something is wrong with it. Do you drink low-fat coffee?>

<There is no such thing as low-fat coffee. There's Deathwish Javambrosia and there's everything else. Besides, we aren't talking about me. I'm not the one putting on the pounds, you are. You keep this up, we're going to need a Dark Truck.>

<I'm growing. Meat is important for me to grow.>

<You're growing alright. Growing sideways. Low-fat meat diet is on the menu for you, boy.>

<A low-fat diet sounds like something the angry man eats. He

is always angry. Do you want me angry? You wouldn't like me when I'm angry.>

I thought about an angry hellhound roaming the streets of New York City. I imagined the devastation and destruction...it was a brief, scary thought.

<*Fine, but we have to find healthy alternatives, or you won't fit in the backseat to do your incredisprawl. At this rate, we'll have to hitch a trailer to the Goat just to lug you around.*>

<*Healthier alternatives sound like the bad meat you made. That almost broke my stomach and made the bad air. Do you want bad air?*>

I shook my head.

<*We'll finish this conversation later. For now, I'm telling Ezra to give you half a titanium bowl of pastrami. I need you to be a lean, mean, fighting machine.*>

<*Half a bowl is not enough. It's only a start. I'm going to need presentation, a liar.*>

<*I think you mean representation, a lawyer. For what? Why would a hellhound ever need a lawyer?*>

<*Frank says there are people who fight for my rights. He said hellhounds have rights too. I should shoe you if you don't provide enough meat. That it would be like working in a sweaty shop.*>

<*No more talking to Frank until I have a conversation with that lizard.*>

<*Mage. Frank is a mage.*>

<*He's going to be a smear when I'm finished with him, mage or not.*>

<*He says if you threaten him, he's going to light up your life.*>

<*He said that? He threatened me?*>

<*I don't think it was a threat. He said he would give you the jolt of your life. That sounds fun.*>

<We'll see about that, no more talking to the mage lizard until I say so, and half a bowl of meat in order to save the Dark Goat.>

Peaches gave off a low rumble that ended with a small bark, rocking the Dark Goat on its suspension.

"Something the matter with your creature?" Monty asked, glancing into the rear seat. "He seems upset. Does he need meat?"

<Yes!>

"No," I said, looking into the rear-view mirror. "He's getting out of shape as it is. And no, round is not the shape he needs to get into. I need to put him on a low-fat diet."

"Not sure if I can create low-fat sausage," Monty answered, thoughtfully. "I suppose I could give it a try. I'd prefer to avoid another deathane incident. Especially in an enclosed space, like the greater tri-state area."

"We are going to need to stop by The Dive one of these days," I said, letting some menace creep into my voice. "I need to have a conversation with a certain mage lizard."

"Grey and his group are not exactly keen on visitors of the violent sort," Monty said. "If you intend on visiting bodily harm to Frank, I suggest you reconsider. He may look like a lizard, but I can assure you, he is a mage of some ability. The fact that he is alive and in possession of his senses, even after a failed transmogrification, speaks to his considerable skill."

"No bodily harm," I said, shaking my head slowly. "Just a *conversation* about the kind of information he's sharing with my hellhound. This whole Brew and Chew thing is a horrible idea."

"Weren't you saved by Cecelia, two canines—I use the

term canines loosely—and said mage lizard?" Monty asked. "This occurred not too long ago if I recall."

"You mean the young Jotnar ice mage, her guardian-protector-dog-beast, my hellhound, and a mage lizard?" I asked. "I still think it's a horrible idea, even if they did save me."

"I see," Monty said, barely suppressing a smile. "You're upset about your hellhound's association with the very creatures that saved you?"

"That, and if he keeps up the hellhound diet of digestive destruction, the Dark Goat is going to be the Broken Goat," I snapped. "Frank said I have him in sweatshop conditions, and that Peaches should sue me for providing insufficient meat. Sue me? Can you believe that little shit of a lizard?"

"Outrageous," Monty said, barely keeping it together. "The travesty is inconceivable. Can hellhounds even get that sort of legal representation? Sounds like some kind of precedent is involved."

"I'm glad this amuses you," I said. "Are you done with your finger-wiggling?"

"Quite," Monty said with a nod. "The runes have been recalibrated. At least those I could impact. The other runes Cecil inscribed are too dangerous to even attempt to manipulate."

"That always makes me feel safe," I said, starting the engine with a roar. "Are the murdery runes payback for the London Lambo? Is Cecil trying to get back at us?"

"I'm sure he's displeased with the destruction of the vehicle in London. It was an experimental model. An expensive one."

"What was he thinking giving us an experimental

model? Even I wouldn't give us an experimental anything. Especially a Lambo."

"Clearly, he learned his lesson, hence this vehicle with incredibly dangerous and volatile runes," Monty replied. "Good thing he doesn't hold grudges against your destructive tendencies."

"My destructive tendencies? For the record, I didn't get the Goat melted."

"Nor did I."

"Right, the Magistrate just happened to be in the neighborhood and accidentally sent that orb of destruction our way," I said. "It's probably all a huge misunderstanding."

"I wouldn't go that far," Monty said. "Although that orb was excessive."

"Why would Cecil hold a grudge? It was *one* Lamborghini, and it was out of our control."

It was Monty's turn to stare at me.

"Actually it was two Lamborghinis," Monty corrected. "You did destroy one during your ill-fated 'date', if memory serves."

"That wasn't my fault," I said. "The Aventador was blown up by an angry troll, if you recall. Actually, neither one was my fault. The Urus was one of those London tracker demons."

"The tracker demon was not particular to London. I'm sure Cecil installed the new runes to keep us safe from experiencing a fate similar to the first iteration of this vehicle."

"The Goat was melted by your Golden Circle magistrate buddies."

"While the vehicle was in our possession," Monty

added. "I'm sure you could explain all of the details to Cecil."

"No, thanks. He'd probably just add more murder runes."

"I doubt he could," Monty said. "We are driving a veritable runic time bomb. Cecil is serious about trying to destroy the Beast. Or us."

"Or both. So glad we could be his guinea pigs," I said. "I'm really feeling that five star SuNaTran love. Why doesn't he put death runes on his own car? Does he even have a car? I've never seen him drive a vehicle."

"He does," Monty said. "He would never put those runes on his personal vehicle."

"Why?" I asked. "Is it too precious?"

"I'm sure it is, at least to him," Monty answered. "Cecil drives the 1939 Duesenberg Simone Midnight Ghost."

"No way," I said, surprised. "There's only one of those. If the rumors are true. How did he get it?"

"From Simone herself," Monty said. "I've only seen him drive it once. It is truly an automotive work of art."

"He didn't rune it?" I asked. "Can't it get damaged?"

"I didn't say he wouldn't rune it, just that he wouldn't put the runes from our vehicle in the Midnight Ghost," Monty said. "The runes he placed on the Duesenberg makes it indestructible, without the inherent threat of death."

"Oh, he gave us the special 'murder rune' treatment," I grumbled. "That was thoughtful."

"I'm certain he felt justified, considering our past treatment of his vehicles."

Cecil had made some major adjustments to the Dark Goat besides the scary murder runes that gave off a distinct 'I will devour your soul' vibe. Olga had initially notified us that all of the parking attendants from the building garage refused to go near the Dark Goat, but we didn't know how serious it was.

I didn't blame them.

Christine felt like a family-friendly car compared to the Dark Goat. The runes in and on it gave off a seriously angry, menacing energy. Every time I got behind the wheel, the energy in the vehicle felt like an army of fire ants gently chewing into my skin. On a good day.

Once I started the engine, the sensation dissipated, but I couldn't imagine any of the attendants dealing with that feeling for longer than a few seconds. The fact that one of them tried to drive the Dark Goat, sounded like they were hazing the new guy.

That was a mistake.

I made sure to inform Olga that no one was to try and drive the Dark Goat, citing it was a rare classic, and I didn't want any damage to it. The truth was if anyone besides me tried to drive it, they'd be removing the lifeless body of the daring parking attendant from behind the wheel.

The new guy was lucky.

Olga didn't buy the 'rare classic' line and narrowed her eyes at the Dark Goat when she went down to resolve the attendants' boycott about parking it. I had to tell her some of the truth, realizing she could see the murder runes Cecil had graced the exterior of the Goat with.

Her disapproval was clear when I informed her about some of the real dangers of anyone else trying to drive the Dark Goat. Shortly thereafter, Olga designated one of the corners of the garage as our parking space.

The new parking space was clearly demarcated with bright, safety orange designators, cones, and a thick chain attached to the walls. The Dark Goat was separated with plenty of space—enough for three vehicles— from all the other cars in the garage.

"You park and drive yourself, Stronk," she said, with the usual mangling of my name while giving me a glare. *"No kill my employees with your demon car."*

We sped out of the garage and headed to Ezra's.

FIFTEEN

"How exactly is Ezra going to point us in the right direction?" I asked, swerving around traffic. "I mean, I know he's Death, but what does that have to do with Fate?"

"Nothing, at the moment," Monty answered. "I would imagine that he does, however, have a connection to Kali. Even if it is an indirect one."

"Why? She's the goddess of destruction, not death."

"She is very similar to the Morrigan in many respects," Monty said. "The aspect that I think pertains to our current situation, is her aspect as a form of Death."

"You're thinking they could have a Death-to-Death conversation?" I asked, feeling slightly confused. "Is Ezra *the* Death or just one of the many forms Death takes to deal with humans?"

"I don't think many people interact with Ezra in that form as Death," Monty answered. "Somehow, sitting in a deli and appearing as a Jewish scholar, doesn't strike me as an ideal form for dispatching humans from this life."

"At least you'd get an awesome lunch as your last meal...

the place has sandwiches that could stop your heart," I said. "Just from the amount of pastrami stuffed into them."

"I think it's a selling point, but an awkward method of ushering one into the afterlife."

"True," I said, narrowly missing a yellow taxi that wanted to trade paint with the Dark Goat...a losing proposition for said cab. "It's not like Death is going to invite you out to lunch, then poof...you're gone."

"Seems a little inconvenient, I think," Monty said. "I'm sure he takes on a different form. One more practical for final meetings."

"Black robe, skull head, and sickle, then?"

"Death appears to us as we need him to, I think," Monty said. "Like Fate or Karma, Death is a being independent of gender and exists outside time. I'm sure he could adopt many different forms."

"Yet he sits in a deli, studying old books and providing pastrami for my hellhound," I said. "I'm going to ask him why."

"Why he sits in a deli?"

"Why he appears as an old scholar *and* sits in a deli," I said. "Maybe it's the food?"

"Do you think Ezra *needs* to eat?"

"Probably not, but the food in the deli is incredible, I'd go so far as to say it's *deli*cious," I said. "See what I did there? That's called creative wordplay."

"Staggering," Monty replied. "Did you tax your brain cell to come up with that one?"

"Jealousy doesn't suit you," I said. "I know you wish you could handle words with my expertise."

"It's on my mind every waking moment," Monty deadpanned. "How you manage to exacerbate the danger of precarious situations into the realms of immediate lethality, with just your words. Boggles the imagination."

"I'll teach you one day."

"Let me check my schedule and see when I can fit that lesson in. The day after never seems about right."

"Hilarious," I said, looking up at the entrance of Ezra's. "Maybe Ezra just likes being around the energy of the place? It's always a bustle of activity. Could be all that life attracts Death."

"How philosophical," Monty said. "I doubt you'll get an answer you can comprehend. The best we could hope for is a good meal and a cryptic response, knowing Ezra."

We parked outside of Katz's Deli on 1st Avenue. I never worried about the Dark Goat being ticketed, towed, or tampered with. Aside from the locks Cecil installed, which made it impervious to theft, the murder runes on the chassis gave anyone who stepped too close the immediate desire of sprinting away, and screaming while doing so.

In addition, Ramirez had placed a DNA-Do Not Approach warning on it. The Dark Goat was one of only two vehicles in the city, to my knowledge, with such a warning. The other belonged to Grey and his Beast of a Camaro. Now, *that* car was seriously scary.

My best Zilleresque guess, after giving it some thought, was that Katz's Deli and Ezra's Place shared the same inter-dimensional space, but on parallel planes. You entered the one appropriate to your power level when you crossed the threshold. I was cursed alive, Monty wielded insane amounts of energy, and Peaches was...well, Peaches,

I doubted we would ever enter the 'real' Katz's Deli when we crossed the entrance to the deli.

We got out of the Dark Goat. I placed a hand on it, causing the runes along its surface to flash orange as the sound of anvils being struck clanged, activating the locks, and securing it in place.

"Why does Cecil bother placing locks on his vehicles? Especially *this* vehicle."

"Pardon?" Monty said. "Locks are a prudent deterrent from theft."

"If someone—or, in the Dark Goat's case—something, was tampering with it, I don't think the locks are going to be our main concern. Getting away in one piece would probably be the priority in that situation."

Monty paused to look at the Dark Goat and nodded.

"Agreed," he said. "In this case, it's probably to prevent mishap to an unsuspecting car thief."

"That *would* be a bad day. Try and break into the Dark Goat, get your brain fried by a car. Are we certain it's not sentient?"

"The last thing I want to consider is a sentient mode of transportation," Monty said, stepping away from the Dark Goat. "Especially this mode."

"Just saying, with all those runes Cecil added, I'm surprised he hasn't transformed it into some kind of Dark Goat being of destruction. Although, that would be badass."

Monty stared at me for a second.

"Actually, no. It wouldn't."

"It totally would, but then we'd probably need to destroy it," I said, lightly tapping the hood of the Dark Goat. "Better if she's just a car. A very scary car."

"Indeed. Let's go see Ezra. We're on a schedule."

The runes along the threshold to the deli flared orange as we stepped inside.

The first thing I noticed was the noise. Ezra's was a chaotic jumble of conversation, clanging dinnerware and yelled out orders from the front counter to the kitchen in the back. It was a small sample of the energy of the city, just this side of full blown madness.

I loved it.

For all intents and purposes, this *was* Katz's, with the exception that the patrons were a mix of mages and beings of incredible power.

Some I could sense right away; others, like Fate, felt like pockets of emptiness, a void within the space of excess energy. I made sure to keep an eye on those, and gave them space as we made our way to Ezra's table in the corner.

Some of them gazed in my direction with a disinterested air. The same way I would look at a spider crawling on the wall. Vaguely interesting...capable of being crushed with a swipe if need be.

Walking into Ezra's always filled me with a sense of the familiar. That, no matter what happened in my currently chaos filled life, this place would never change. The energy of the deli was vibrant, with servers moving between tables, taking orders with speed and efficiency.

The decor hadn't changed in the slightest. Photos of celebrities covered the walls. Small tables, which sat four, filled most of the floor space. Some of the tables were occupied with patrons either eating or having lively conversations. A large wooden counter ran across one wall with men, who were serving food and drinks, behind it. I noticed that some of the photos were unfamiliar.

We weaved around the servers and patrons, making it to the corner where Ezra usually sat. I thought about how to frame a request for half a bowl of pastrami, knowing there was a good chance he would veto my request.

I had a feeling Ezra belonged to the school of oversized portions of food. We never discussed current situations without eating, and we never left his place without extra food to go. A half bowl of pastrami could be seen as an insult if I asked the wrong way.

We made it to the corner of the deli and I stopped suddenly, surprised. I looked around to make sure we were in the right corner.

Ezra's table was empty.

SIXTEEN

"He's not here?" I asked, looking around, confused. "Since when does Ezra leave this place?"

"I'm certain he must from time to time," Monty said, glancing behind the counter and raising a hand. "This must be one of those times."

"To do what? Check out a book from the library?"

"I doubt any of the books he reads would be found in a local library, or any library for that matter," Monty said as a server approached us. "I'm sure he is powerful enough to materialize any book he needs."

"True," I said, "but what would need his *actual* presence? This feels wrong."

"This way, please," the server said. "The Miss will be with you in a second."

It took my brain a second to process the word that sounded like 'meese'. Once it did, I realized he meant 'Miss'. His thick accent, was more at home in Piero's than Ezra's. With a gesture, he directed us to a table.

"The Miss?" I muttered to Monty as we followed the server. "Who's the Miss?"

The server led us through the maze of tables and patrons, with the practiced expertise of flawless navigation, and sat us at Ezra's table. It felt strange sitting there without Ezra. I was used to seeing him sitting at the table, reading a book and beckoning us to take a seat as he chastised us for not eating enough.

"What would you like?" the server asked as we sat at the table. "The usual?"

"Huh? Yes please, the usual," I said, still shocked at Ezra's absence. "Only half a bowl of pastrami for Peaches."

"This is not the usual," the server said with a huff. "The boss said to always give the puppy a full bowl"—the server glanced down at Peaches—"half a bowl and he will leave hungry. This is not acceptable. A hungry hellhound is a dangerous hellhound."

"Excuse me?" I said. "What's your name?"

"My name is Anton, Mr. Strong."

He said Anton with emphasis, making the second half of the name sound like 'tone' for a full effect of 'Ahntone'. The French accent clashed with the context of the deli, but this was Ezra's. Anything was possible.

"Okay, Anton," I said with the same intonation. "You must be new here, but—"

"No sir, I have been in the employ of this establishment since the Blitzkrieg," Anton said. "The boss left specific instructions regarding the portions allocated to Monsieur Pêches."

"What's a peshis?" I asked, looking at Monty who was doing his best to ignore me. "His name is—"

"Pêches," Anton answered. "Your companion, excuse me... his name is Peaches."

I glared at Monty, who was deliberately looking away and suppressing a smile, before turning my attention back to Anton.

"The Blitzkrieg?" I asked. "You don't look a day over thirty."

"Merci," Anton said with a short bow. "I must insist on a full bowl, along with your pastrami on rye with an egg cream."

I looked down at my ever-hungry hellhound. He was doing his best puppy eyes and terrifying grin.

<Stop that before you scare everyone out of here.>

<Would that mean more meat for me?>

<No, it would mean we would have to leave without meat.>

<Should I speak?>

<No! I mean, no. I got this, thanks. No help needed. The situation is under control.>

<Should I call Frank? He can get me more meat if I ask.>

<Don't you dare...wait a minute what do you mean 'call Frank'?>

"Sir?" Anton asked, interrupting my thoughts. "Full bowl, yes?"

"It's just that he's putting on the pounds and—"

"Anton does make sense," Monty said, cutting me off. "Perhaps you could alter your creature's diet later on, when we aren't facing more pressing matters?"

"The only matter that's pressing will be Peaches when he doesn't fit in the Dark Goat."

"You do realize he can alter his size?"

"I've only seen normal and XL, and his normal is slowly *becoming* XL."

"Please take a moment," Anton interjected, looking at Monty. "Salad as always, sir?"

Monty nodded.

"Yes, please, thank you."

I realized this wasn't a battle I could win or was willing to fight. If I insisted, and word got back to Ezra, he would accuse me of trying to starve my hellhound. I would never hear the end of it.

"Sir?" Anton said, looking at me again. "The usual?"

"Fine, the usual. Do you have healthy pastrami?"

Anton raised an eyebrow and gave me a look that said 'clearly you must have smacked your head on the door coming in' before shaking his head slowly.

"We have pastrami and pastrami," he said. "All our pastrami is good for you *and* healthy. I will bring you all the usual."

He gave us another short bow, stepped back and headed away.

"Why did I even bother to ask?" I asked, as Anton sped away before I could make another request. "He's as bad as Ezra."

"I don't believe there is a healthy alternative to pastrami," Monty said. "At least not here."

"Sure there is," I countered. "Didn't you hear Anton? There's pastrami and pastrami. Everything is healthy."

"I believe that's called sarcasm," Monty said. "Besides, Ezra won't allow you to change 'the usual' in his absence."

"Or in his presence," I said. "He always tells us what we need to eat when we visit."

"Because in many cases he knows you better than you know yourself," a voice said from behind us. "He is, after all, Death."

It was Mori.

Mori, Death's PA, grabbed a chair and joined us at the table, stretching out her long legs. She was tall, and dressed in what I imagined was the combat-casual version of Ezra's outfit. Her dual shoulder holsters, which usually held two hand cannons, were missing.

She still wore the black Kevlar vest minus the magazines of extra ammo. Under the vest, she wore a starched, white, dragonscale dress shirt, black pants, and finished off the ensemble with a pair of black Dr. Martens steel-toed Hynines.

"You're unarmed?" I asked. "Is this the new manager look?"

"I'm never unarmed. The guns"—she said, extending a hand, materializing one of her handcannons, and placing it on the table—"make some of the customers nervous, or so I'm told."

"Got it," I said, eyeing the large weapon. "This is combat casual, then. Where's Ezra?"

"I apologize for not greeting you when you entered," Mori said. "We had an issue in the kitchen. Never fails when the old man steps out."

"Steps out?" I asked. "Since when does Ezra 'step out'?"

She pushed up the pair of glasses on the bridge of her nose and stared at me.

"Do you really think he spends every moment in here?" Mori asked, narrowing her eyes at me. "What did you do?"

"What do you mean? I didn't do anything."

"Your energy"—she waved a hand in my direction—"is all over the place. You're even more of a chaotic mess than usual. No offense."

"None taken. We need to find Kali," I said. "Can you help us?"

"Have you grown tired of living?" Mori asked. "Because that has to be one of the worst ideas I've heard today."

Below us, Peaches rumbled at Mori.

Mori looked down and rubbed his head.

"Have you been a good boy?" she singsonged to him. "Did you learn your lessons? Have you eaten?"

"I don't think any of his lessons stuck, really," I said. "None that mattered anyway."

"Sure they did," Mori said, still rubbing Peaches' head. "He hasn't turned enormous and tried to destroy the city. I'd call that a win with a hellhound."

"Anton insisted on a full bowl of meat for him."

"Those are the instructions," Mori said serious. "No one is going to do otherwise while Ezra is away."

"Or while he's here."

"True. The old man is kind of set in his ways," Mori said after a pause, and looked down at Peaches again. "Besides, he's still a puppy and he needs his meat. He's a growing boy."

<Does she have meat?>

<You have meat coming. Can you wait?>

<I can eat meat while I wait for the meat. That is called multiple tasking.>

<It's multi-tasking, and that is not what it is. Eating meat while waiting for meat is just called overeating.>

<I've never heard of that. How can anyone overeat? Are they sick?>

<No, they just don't think about meat every second of every day.>

<Sounds like a very sad life. Ask her for some meat before

meat. Horror doors is what Frank calls them. Says all the good food places have them. You just have to ask. Can you ask her?>

<Hors d'oeuvres and no. You're getting a titanium bowl full of meat. Waiting won't kill you. Delayed gratification is good for you.>

<Delayed gratification sounds painful. Do you do it?>

<All the time. Right now, I'm doing it for you. No horror doors.>

<I don't think I like delayed gratification.>

<It's good for you. Settle down while your food arrives.>

"Where did Ezra go?" Monty asked. "We have an urgent matter to discuss with him."

SEVENTEEN

"He's out," Mori said. "I can't say more than that."

"That's pretty vague," I said. "Can't or won't?"

"Both," Mori replied, reabsorbing the gun from the table into into her hand. "Maybe I can help you?"

"We need to locate and contact Kali," Monty said. "It's urgent."

"It better be if you're reaching out to her," Mori said, looking at me. "Does this have to do with his messy energy signature?"

"Yes," Monty said. "It would seem Simon has managed to discover a method to disrupt causality."

"Whoa," I said, raising a hand. "This isn't something I 'managed' to do. This was a side effect."

"Your side effect is breaking reality?" Mori asked. "A side effect of what?"

"Being exposed to too much runic energy," I said. "At least that's the best guess according to Monty."

"That doesn't make sense," Mori said. "You've barely

been exposed to any serious amounts of energy. Trust me on this."

"I've dealt with a fair amount of gods and creatures," I said. "Isn't that exposure?"

"You've dealt with these gods and creatures in a form that kept your brain from melting, not in their true forms. *That* would be overexposure."

"Then how am I breaking reality?" I asked, turning to Monty. "How am I 'upsetting the balance'?"

"A good question," Monty said. "Your signature is quite off, but it's possible there may be another cause for the disturbance."

"The Force?"

Monty gave me a two on the glare-o-meter.

"What force?" Mori asked. "There's a force?"

"No, there isn't," Monty answered before I could expound. "There is no force."

"Why would she lie?" I asked. "Something smells off."

<It wasn't me. I smell wonderful.>

<I didn't say it was you.>

<You are the one that smells different.>

<I know. It's my energy signature.>

<You need more meat. That will help your smelling.>

<I doubt meat is the solution to my problem. I'm not a hellhound.>

<But you are my bondmate. Meat is the solution.>

<I think that is an opinion of one.>

<I haven't eaten yet. Is the meat coming soon?>

<Yes, just be patient.>

"I'm missing something. Why do you want to see Kali then?" Mori asked. "Just find a way to not break reality. I know...*not* breaking something may be an alien concept for you two, but it's possible. One second, who lied?"

Monty explained the meeting with Fate, and Mori's face darkened.

"Are you sure it was Fate?" Mori asked, placing both hands on the table and staring at me. "How do you do this?"

"Do what?"

"Get the attention of these nasty beings of power," Mori said. "Did you make sure it was Fate?"

"No, I didn't make sure," I snapped. "It's not like she walked around with a name tag or ID. She said she was Fate, managed to be inside our office, past our heavy duty security and gave off a serious void vibe. It's not like I've met Fate before."

"Tristan?" Mori asked. "Your impression?"

"She was powerful, whoever she was," Monty said, steepling his fingers and resting his elbows on the table. "Like Simon said, she bypassed our security and exuded a considerable amount of power. At least on par with Hades."

"She wanted you to become mortal again?" Mori asked. "To supposedly restore balance to—?"

"Everything?" I said. "She was big on the whole balance thing, and how it was my fault everything was out of whack."

"This doesn't make sense," Mori said, tapping her lip with a finger. "Fate has no reason to visit you. Your immortality was a surprise, but not something that would upset causality, especially not from runic exposure."

"Are you saying she was lying?" I asked, suddenly angry at being played. "She wasn't really Fate?"

"I don't know who or what she was, but think about this. Why would Fate need *you* to restore balance? Fate is powerful enough to be close to the old man's league. Why would she need your help?"

"Because of my condition?" I said. "I am cursed alive, you know."

"Hate to burst your bubble, O immortal one," Mori said with a small chuckle. "Even the gods give her space. She isn't infallible, and she isn't inevitable like the old man, but beings of power give her a wide berth. Why reach out to you?"

"True, we can change our fates," I said. "We can alter our lives. Which must happen constantly...every choice is a different path."

"Exactly," Monty said. "Unless she needs a specific outcome."

"Then why single me out?"

"That is the question," Mori said. "Why you? It's not like immortality is remarkable, considering the circles you both move in. There is more going on here. Which of the three did you speak to?"

"She said she was Lachesis in triune form," Monty answered. "I asked her why weren't we speaking to Atropos."

"What did she say?"

"She didn't," I answered. "She said something about not being able to cut my thread, but deflected Monty's question with some not-so-subtle threats about erasing everyone my life touched."

"Fate wouldn't need to threaten you," Mori said. "Fate is a being of destiny. She just is. Like Death. The old man doesn't need to threaten anyone. Eventually, they all meet him. Fate kind of operates the same way."

"Except you can change your destiny," I said. "By your force of will and action."

"Or have it changed for you," Mori said. "By a pissed off goddess."

"Fate made real emphasis on my having to be mortal again. That part was important."

"Who or what stands to gain by you becoming mortal?" Mori asked. "I mean, besides the property value of the city?"

"I think the question is: who does Simon threaten, as an immortal?" Monty asked. "Who is being thwarted by his presence?"

"Do you still want to speak to Kali?" Mori asked. "She may have the answers you need. I sure don't."

"Yes," I said after a few seconds of thought. "Kali is still the goddess of creation, right? I mean, she cursed me alive. She could have blasted me to atoms, but didn't."

"You really think that was the better of the two options?" Mori asked. "Kali has a tendency to lean toward the destruction side of things, but you're right. She may have the answers you need."

"I have a question," I said. "About Ezra. Is he *the* Death? How did you become his PA? Are you two the same being?"

"That's three questions."

"Can you answer them?"

"Sure," Mori said with a wicked smile. "Yes, none of your business, and no."

"That was helpful," I said. "No need to be so touchy."

"You still don't understand basic etiquette when dealing with beings of power."

"Basic etiquette?" I asked, confused. "Those were simple questions."

"Far from it," Mori said. "When you are dealing with a BOP-being of power, be excruciatingly specific. Vague questions can get you all kinds of unpleasantness, and loopholes can quickly become nooses. Remember that."

"I will. Still won't answer the questions?"

"Fine," Mori said with a short sigh. "Only because I know you won't let this go."

"You're right, I won't."

"Ezra is a personification of Death," Mori started. "For your level of understanding right now, he is Death, capital D. Ask me again once you've lived a few millennia. How I became his PA? I made a deal with him. One that is personal and will not be shared at this moment. As far as us being the same being, I have a question for you: Are you the same as Kali?"

"Well, no," I said. "She cursed me alive, but I'm not her. I'm not a god."

"You've answered your question then. If you really want to go see Kali, you need to go to this address."

Mori grabbed a pad and wrote down an address, sliding it across the table.

"Kali lives in Jersey?" I asked, looking down at the address. "Seriously?"

"Has he suffered head trauma?" Mori asked Monty. "Something severe?"

"Are you asking if it was recent," Monty asked, "or during his formative years?"

"Oh, the hilarity," I said. "You should both take your show on the road. Start down south, like Antartica."

"The doors to Kali's domain are thinner at certain locations," Mori said. "That address will lead you to one of the doors. I can't guarantee she'll be happy to see you though."

"I have that effect on people," I said. "What's the worse she can do? She already cursed me alive."

"There are some things worse than dying, Simon," Mori said. "If you don't know this by now, you'll learn it soon enough."

I was about to answer when Anton appeared with our meal. Two more servers walked behind him, one carrying an enormous bowl of pastrami, the other carrying the rest of the food. The first server hefted the pastrami bowl and placed it under the table for Peaches with a grunt. They left the food, bowed silently and stepped away from the table.

"Thank you," I said to Anton and crew. Mori gave him a nod of approval and they left. "I know there are worse things than death and dying, but it's time I confront her about why she did what she did to me."

"You think she's going to lift the curse?" Mori asked gently. "This is Kali. She may be the goddess of creation, but she knows how to hold a grudge. You got her angry enough to curse you, something few have managed to achieve and survive."

"We kind of disrupted an op she had going on," I said. "One that was 500 years in the making."

"You still want to go visit her?" Mori asked, standing while shaking her head slowly. "Maybe get your affairs in order first?"

"That's encouraging," I said, suddenly hungry with the

smell of pastrami on rye wafting up to my nose. “Maybe she’ll be in a good mood when I see her.”

Mori laughed.

“Good luck,” she said. “I hope this isn’t the last time I see you...alive.”

EIGHTEEN

"I'm starving," I said, as I took a bite of the sandwich tempting me. "What do you think?"

"About you starving?" Monty asked. "Unlikely. You're almost as bad as your creature when it comes to eating. Bottomless."

"About what Mori said...that it wasn't really Fate."

"I'm not sure," Monty said, placing a napkin across his lap. "This opens many possibilities. You have made many enemies in your short time as an immortal."

"I've made? You're the mage."

"She wasn't there to see me," Monty corrected with an extended index finger. "She was specifically there to see *you*."

"If it wasn't Fate, then who was it? Scary beings of power is more your department."

"How is this my department?" Monty said, slowly skewering some salad with his fork. "You've made angering gods an art form."

"You're the mage," I said, around a mouthful of

pastrami. "Isn't there a list of super beings and what they look like? Some kind of directory?"

"Of course," Monty said with a nod. "Why didn't I think of that earlier? It comes complete with emails, likes, dislikes, favorite foods, and colors too. I'll just look up Fate and see if her picture matches."

"A simple no would've been enough, you know," I said, shaking my head. "Less is more."

"We need to go see Roxanne," Monty said, after eating some of his salad. "Despite what Fate said—if it was Fate—your condition is serious and Roxanne may have some insight."

"If you recall *that* was my suggestion before the torture you called a test happened," I answered. "We could have avoided all my agony."

"Once you eliminate the impossible, whatever remains no matter how improbable..."

"Must be the truth," I finished. "I get that, really. What impossibility did we eliminate with my torture? Aside from the fact that you're a closet mad scientist, and I'm somehow affecting reality around me?

"Several things, actually," Monty said, holding up a finger. "You aren't a mage."

"Wow, it took you this long to figure that one out?"

"Let me finish," Monty said, scowling. "Even though you aren't a mage, you have the potential to be one...a powerful one."

"Pass. We've had this discussion," I said, shaking my head. "I don't do the finger waving or manipulation of major energy. Did you forget the orb on the Strix? I'm sure René hasn't."

"No, no one has," Monty agreed. "Or your 'magic

missiles' as you call them. I'm not referring to that, but rather the potentiality of your inherent power. Haven't you ever wondered why Kali cursed you, or why your vampire gave you the blade?"

"You mean aside from the fact that I pissed off Kali and interrupted her op, or that Michiko is just beyond my understanding? No."

"It's possible that Kali cursed you because of that latent power, which resulted in your vampire giving you the blade for safekeeping."

I had thought of it, actually. It was a rabbit hole I tried to avoid. Admitting I had this power meant I had to take responsibility for it. I didn't want the power or the responsibility, not in this or any lifetime.

"Not really," I lied. "I just figured they hated me and wanted to make my life as miserable as possible."

"You realize that with great power comes..."

"I swear if you Uncle Ben me, I'm going to unleash a magic missile in your direction, right here and right now."

Monty raised a hand in surrender.

"I was merely pointing out that the possibility of your inherent power could've been the prime motivator for Kali, your vampire, and even Hades who entrusted you with your creature."

"What's the alternative suggestion?"

"That you just irk everyone you meet, and they wish you the utmost harm immediately upon hearing you speak?"

"Sounds harsh, but doesn't that make more sense?"

"Not really," Monty countered. "Yes, you are annoying and ill-mannered, with little to no filter on your thoughts or words, but—"

"Why don't you tell me how you really feel?"

"But,"—he pointed at my chest—"Nana made you my shield-bearer," He let the words hang for a few seconds. "Uncle Dex trusts you, and dare I say, even likes you. He barely tolerates me."

"You are a bit stuffy, you know," I replied. "I don't understand how you two are even related."

"Both of them are excellent judges of character," Monty continued, ignoring me. "I trust their judgment, and you have demonstrated more than once that you are honorable, even if you are impetuous."

"I'm not impetuous," I said. "I just act on my impulses, sometimes without thinking first."

"Precisely," Monty answered. "Their actions lend credence to the potentiality of overwhelming power postulate."

"The what? C'mon, did you just make that up?"

"Preposterous," he snapped. "The first mention of the Potentiality Of Overwhelming Power Postulate pre-dates even Professor Ziller. I can assure you I did not 'make up' its existence."

"I'm sorry I asked," I said. "You realize that it's the postulate of poop, right?"

"Only to your brain," Monty answered, shaking his head. "Are you going to let me finish or is this where your puerile remarks take over?"

"Please," I said, waving him on. "Tell me all about the postulate of poop. Does it smell?"

"In any case," Monty continued past my answer, doing his best to maintain his composure. Mages were so easy to rile. "The potentiality of overwhelming power postulate states that power in its inherent form is neutral. Neither good or bad, just dormant or active."

"We both know that's not entirely true," I said, mental red flags going up. "I've seen power used for evil. We both have."

"True, but the power itself wasn't evil, merely its expression."

I didn't like where this conversation was going. It was a slippery slope. An argument used by those who would pervert power to commit acts of unspeakable evil. Or... dark mages excusing their use of blood magic.

"I would argue that using power to commit evil or darkness, makes it evil or dark, not neutral."

"The world isn't black and white, Simon," Monty said. "There are many shades of gray, especially when it comes to wielding power. Something you yourself have confessed...you aren't a mage. You know little of manipulating vast amounts of power with a gesture or a word."

"I know actions, Monty," I countered, letting the concern seep into my voice as I stared at him...hard. "Actions speak louder than words. A mage uses dark magic enough times"—the example was deliberate—"and eventually it becomes easier and easier to use. Before you know it, the mage becomes Lord Overbearing of the Outer Darkness, controlling, enslaving, and killing people. I've yet to meet the Dark Mage of Good Intentions. They may start out that way, but it's not where they end up."

"I am not a dark mage," Monty said, his words low and dangerous. "Nor will I ever become one."

"Never said you were," I said. "I'm just saying power isn't neutral in my book. Power corrupts and absolute power corrupts absolutely. You said it: Nana made *me* your shield-bearer. Part of *my* job is to make sure you stay away from the dark side. Bad enough mages all dress at Sith Fashions."

"Duly noted. More to the point however, your inherent power and its impact on reality or causality as we know it, has gotten attention."

"The wrong kind of attention, if you ask me."

"Not wrong or right," Monty said. "Just attention."

"From beings of power like a pseudo-Fate? Which explains this morning's visit."

"By beings who would subvert its use, and subject you, to their own agenda."

"In this case, the agenda feels nefarious," I said. "Fate didn't say she wanted me mortal so she could restore balance to end world hunger. It sounded more like she wanted me out of the way. Mortal and killable."

"Be that as it may, the being who appeared in our office may have tipped her hand," Monty said. "The one-week threat was melodramatic, but revealing."

"All it revealed was that I have a week to get this situation resolved. Melodrama or not. She had the energy signature to back up her threat. I felt it and so did you."

"Indeed," Monty said with a nod. "But why a week? What happens in a week?"

"You mean besides Ms. Pseudo-Fate showing up to blast the people in my life to dust?"

"Yes, besides that, obviously."

"Don't know," I said with a shrug. "What I do know is that she isn't going to touch the people in my life...not without a fight. Did we learn *anything* that could help us at that Hunter's Keep?"

"We *were* able to get important information from the

phasic scan," Monty said. "Even though your creature interrupted the end process."

"Are you referring to the moment when he saved me?" I asked. "I thought all seven rings activated?"

"That's just it," Monty said. "They weren't supposed to. You aren't a mage, which is why I thought the process would proceed smoothly."

"Sure, that clears it all up...not," I said. "Explain."

"By not being a mage, the third ring should have been the highest ring activated," Monty answered. "A seventh ring phasic scan should have been impossible. Much less you surviving it. It means you possess more power than I thought. It would be that increase that has made you so popular."

"Oh wonderful," I said with a groan. "Why can't I attract a being of infinite coffee goodness and deep tissue massages?"

"Your vampire would probably have an opinion about you meeting with that being...a violent opinion," Monty said. "Besides, no such being exists."

"As far as you know."

"As far as *anyone* knows, actually. Do you really think a being like that would be kept secret?"

"Good point. This is why you believed our guest was Fate," I said. "The results of the phasic scan aligned with what she said about my disrupting causality."

"Initially," he answered, after chewing and dabbing one side of his mouth. "But do you recall what I said?"

"Honestly? I'm tuning you out half the time," I answered, after devouring the last of my sandwich, and leaning back totally and completely full. "The other half, I barely understand the words escaping your mouth."

"Splendid, I said that she said something relevant," Monty replied. "She said—"

"No one escapes or alters their fate, no one," I said. "I remember."

"You *were* paying attention...good. Then it stands to reason that Fate, the *real* Fate, wouldn't be coming to *you* for help. You couldn't stop Fate even if you tried."

"I don't believe in fate," I said. "I choose my destiny, not some distant being. Me. My choices, my actions, decide my fate."

"But you do believe in Karma?"

"I've seen her in action," I said, rubbing a jaw. "One does not piss off Karma. She is the most patient bitch I know. I mean that in the most flattering and scary sense possible."

I hedged my bets just in case she was in the neighborhood, eavesdropping.

"I would imagine her methods are thorough," Monty said. "Which contradicts the behavior of our guest this morning."

"So we're dealing with a fake Fate?" I asked, not really understanding the logic. "Why is someone with that much power pretending to be Fate? Of all the entities why pick that one? That's pretty bad."

"Worse, we're dealing with an entity that could bypass my defenses as if they didn't exist, and can mask their signature almost completely," Monty answered with a frown...well, a deeper than usual frown. "That can only mean one thing."

"We've pissed off someone who wants us gone?"

"No...well yes, in theory," Monty corrected. "Someone who wants *you*, the immortal you, out of the way."

"Do we really need to go see Kali?" I asked, suddenly rethinking the entire trip to visit a goddess of destruction. "We could figure this thing out without her help, I think."

"Is that fear I hear in your voice?" Monty asked after finishing his salad. "You are, after all, the 'Chosen of Kali' aren't you?"

"Hell yes, it's fear," I shot back. "She wasn't the one that came up with that title, I'm sure. She probably sees me as the Hemorrhoid of Kali."

"Colorful, but probably accurate," Monty affirmed. "I doubt she holds you in a position of high esteem, much less her 'chosen' anything."

"My thoughts exactly," I said. "We only really met once, and trust me, she made quite the impression; it wasn't one of warmth and kindness."

"I recall," Monty said. "I was there, remember?"

"So we nix the Kali trip?"

"No, think about it," Monty said with a head shake. "She is the perfect one to offer you assistance."

"I think you and I have different ideas about what 'assistance' means," I said. "Every thought I'm having regarding Kali leads to pain and death...Elaborate."

"Fate, or whoever it was, clearly knows about your connection to Kali," Monty started. "They referred to your curse in no uncertain terms. It stands to reason that if they know about Kali then..."

"Kali may know about this fake Fate," I finished. "We can't get that information without paying Kali a visit? Give her a call, shoot her an email, maybe?"

"Somehow, I think a goddess of her stature would be beyond regular technology," Monty said. "However if you have her number, perhaps we should call her?"

"You know very well I don't have her number," I answered. "But this is Kali, I'm sure it's something catchy like 1-800-DESTROY."

"I'm not understanding your trepidation," Monty said, raising a Spockian eyebrow. "It's not like you haven't faced gods or goddesses before. Most of the time, they want to actively, vehemently even, obliterate you, but you haven't shied away from confronting them."

"True, but this one—"

"Is it the potential for mind numbing, excruciating pain, beyond your imagination or description?" Monty mused. "You're practically an expert in pain management by now; a little more shouldn't faze you."

"Your mad scientist is showing again," I said. "It's not the pain, but thanks for the reminder. It's—"

"I highly doubt she can curse you further," Monty continued. "Although, she is a powerful goddess. She could probably double or add conditions to your curse, making it more pronounced. I'll have to study that aspect of divine curses: amplification and modification of curse conditions and their expression."

"Sounds like a wonderful afternoon of brain-melting," I scoffed. "Glad I could give you study material, but that's not it."

"Then what is it?" Monty asked, throwing up a hand. "Where is this fear coming from?"

"It's loss," I admitted. "Loss."

"Sorry? I think you lost me there."

"Exactly, I would lose the only family I have," I said. "Peaches, Roxanne, Michiko, Dex, LD, TK, even you. I would lose the only world I know, my world, everything."

"Glad to see I made the list," Monty said with a brief smile. "But I think I understand."

"Do you?" I asked. "If she wants, she can remove the curse and then blow me away. Can *you* stop her?"

"No...I can't. I could try, but I would fail spectacularly," Monty said after a short moment of silence. "If it's any consolation, I don't think any being could stop her, if she really wanted to follow that course of action."

"That's really encouraging."

"Among deities, Kali is held in great esteem and in even greater fear. No one would dare oppose her. I doubt few could, except maybe Shiva, and we saw how that ended."

"Not so good for him."

"Exactly, few in their right mind would stand against her with any hope of overcoming that particular goddess."

"But you would oppose her?"

"Correction—no one sane would dare stand against her," Monty said. "I'm sure my uncle, Michiko, Roxanne, LD, TK, your creature, and I would try, but even combined, we would still fail."

"She's that powerful?"

"However powerful you think she is...multiply it a thousandfold," Monty answered. "According to my research, entire pantheons avoid her."

"I didn't realize you were doing research," I said surprised. "Since when?"

"Since she cursed you alive," Monty answered quietly, "Chosen of Kali."

"Now you know why I would rather we solve this one on our own," I said after downing the egg cream. "Besides, after this lunch I'm going to need a few days to recover. I need a nap."

"I correct my earlier statement. You're worse than your creature."

I looked under the table to see a sprawled-out Peaches hugging his empty titanium bowl. He had achieved meat-vana and was snoring away in his pastrami-induced coma.

"No one is that bad," I said with a smile, quickly becoming serious. "There's not much of a choice, is there?"

Monty stared at me for a few seconds before sighing, folding his napkin, and placing it next to his plate, just so.

"You aren't alone, you know," Monty said. "Everyone you mentioned would risk their lives for you, and have in the past. If Kali wanted to strike you down, she's had ample means and opportunity to do so, but hasn't."

"Not exactly convincing, this argument of yours."

"You know we have to go see her," Monty said. "But I understand your reluctance. If you'd like, I'll go see her on my own and—"

It was my turn to stare. I'd like to think I gave him a four out of five on the glare-o-meter, easily achieving the Clint Glint, because he stopped speaking.

"I know you're an unstable mage—"

"I'm *not* unstable. I'm merely trying to respect the inordinate amount of bone-chilling fear you are currently exhibiting, while giving you an opportunity to save face."

"Bone-chilling? Wait a second."

"Evidently, the idea of a bloodcurdling encounter has you paralyzed with horror," Monty said. "I'm sure I can pass on a message when I visit. Anything you'd like me to tell her?"

"I can deliver my own messages thank you."

"I was merely thinking of your delicate constitution," Monty replied, while adjusting his sleeves. "I'd hate for you to have nightmares for the rest of your prolonged life. That would be criminal."

"You're not going to see Kali alone," I said. "That sounds like a suicide mission."

"Dangerous yes, suicide, unlikely," Monty said, brushing off his pants. "Unlike some, I possess tact and have thus far refrained from soiling my undergarments from sheer terror."

"Are you saying I'm scared shitless?"

"If the briefs fit," he shot back. "Staying or going? I'm going."

"You aren't the Chosen One."

"Neither are you," Monty answered. "You're the *Cursed* of Kali, big difference."

"Ouch, doesn't matter," I said. "I'm not letting you go see her alone. You and Kali both sound unstable. I may be the only voice of reason when we meet."

"If that's truly the case, we are in deeper trouble than I thought," Monty said, standing. "I suggest you let me do the talking. Every time you engage these beings, we end up nearly dying."

"Like your method of 'diplomacy before destruction' has netted any positive results," I answered. "I'll keep it civil. It's not like she cursed me, upheaved my entire life, and made me a target for beings out to destroy me or anything."

"Perhaps you *should* stay here," Monty said as stood to leave Ezra's. "I have a feeling this isn't going to go well."

"Give me a moment," I said, peeking under the table. "Unless you'd like to carry a passed-out hellhound?"

"Wake your meat-filled creature," Monty said, without turning as he headed for the door. "I don't think

Ezra would appreciate your beast snoring away the patrons."

I crouched down and patted Peaches on the side slowly, careful not to shock him awake. Last thing I needed was one of his barks tearing through Ezra's. After a few pats, he stirred, waking from whatever meat induced dream he was having.

<Let's go, boy. We need to leave. I think you ate yourself into a meat coma.>

<I was just resting my eyes. I am always ready to go.>

<Sure, the rumbling snores gave away your ever-present state of alertness. Head out.>

Peaches walked ahead of me as we stepped out of Ezra's, setting off the runes at the door as we left.

"I don't know what gave you that impression," I said, unlocking the Dark Goat and catching up to Monty. "Me and Kali, we're just going to have a friendly conversation."

"That's what I'm afraid of."

NINETEEN

We sped up the West Side and headed to the Lincoln Tunnel. The Holland Tunnel, which was closer, was also a parking lot at this time of day. The Lincoln, though congested with traffic, at least moved.

"Who would subject themselves to this every day?" Monty asked, looking at the lines of vehicles on 11th Avenue lining up to enter the tunnel. "This is madness."

"This...is...traffic," I said in my best Leonidas Gerard Butler voice. "Madness is going to Jersey to find a door that leads to a psycho-goddess."

"I strongly urge you not to open with 'psycho-goddess' as a form a greeting."

"Pissed off psycho-goddess?"

"We are going to die, and it will be entirely your fault," Monty said. "Why not let me do the greetings?"

"Chosen of Kali here," I said, pointing to my chest. "I'm sure I can handle a meet and greet. Do you know how many divine beings I've met to date? I got this."

"What I do recall is that every one of those divine

beings wanted to blast you to oblivion shortly after meeting you, Kali included."

"They just didn't get to know the real me."

"Knowing the real you would have only sped up their decision-making process," Monty said. "How *did* you manage to live this long?"

"Skill and charm," I said. "Just wait, Kali and I will hit it off."

"I seriously doubt that," Monty replied as his phone rang. "It's Roxanne. Restrain yourself."

I waited until he connected the call before screeching the high note of The Police's famous song which emphasized her name. I was no Sting, but I liked to think I was close to the original.

"Please excuse Simon," Monty said with a wince. "He seems to have permanent brain damage."

"It's not permanent," I countered loud enough for Roxanne to hear me. "It comes and goes."

I heard Roxanne respond but I couldn't make out her words.

"When?" Monty asked, ignoring me, his voice suddenly grim. "How far?"

Monty put the call on speakerphone. The sound of rending metal followed by a loud hum and a crash filled the Dark Goat.

"What the heck is that? When did Roxanne start listening to metal?"

"The wards around the facility have activated," Roxanne said. "The defenses have kicked in. There's a... there's an entropic sphere. Tristan, hurry, I'll meet you at the junction."

"Is the sphere active?"

"No, not yet, thank goodness," Roxanne said, hurriedly. "We're evacuating personnel as we speak, but the sphere is covering the entire supernatural wing."

"Is the detention level affected?" Monty asked. "Does the sphere impact that level?"

"The top floors of the detention level are in the sphere. I have a team on their way down to relocate the recent detainees to the lower levels."

"Detainees?" Monty asked. "I thought Haven Detention was empty for the time being, after the last incident."

"You mean *your* last visit?"

"Yes, that."

"It was," Roxanne said. "We had some temporary transfers from Sheol. They were scheduled to leave in a week."

"Since when does Haven do favors for Division 13?" Monty asked. "That's irregular."

"We don't, usually, but this group needed immediate confinement," Roxanne answered. "We were the only facility available who could accommodate."

"Did you say a week?" I asked. "It was specifically a week?"

"Yes," Roxanne answered, as another screech of metal drowned her out. "The containment is being stressed. We're running out of time."

"We're almost there," Monty said. "Stay away from the sphere. No matter what."

"No promises," Roxanne answered. "Our contingencies didn't take this kind of attack into account. Who can even cast one of these things anymore?"

"Don't touch anything," Monty said, his voice tight with emotion as he glanced at me. "We'll be right there."

"We tried augmenting the wards around the junction," Roxanne said, over the commotion. "They're holding, but I don't know for how long. The entire structure is runically unstable, but the sphere seems inert for now."

"Did you see any of them?" Monty asked. "Were any of the Orchid there?"

"Tristan," Roxanne said with a sigh. "They're all gone. This must be the wards reacting to something else. You did make them quite sensitive. Perhaps they were tripped by accident?"

"Unlikely. Did you see any of them?" Monty asked again, this time his voice hard. "Answer me."

"No, of course not," Roxanne answered, clipping her words. "They're all dead. The Black Orchid was wiped out during the war. You should know this...you...you were there."

"Some may have survived," Monty said. "We survived."

"We had help, remember that," Roxanne said. "It wasn't your fault. That blood is not on your hands."

"We're on our way," I said, accelerating the Dark Goat. "Hold on."

"Call me if anything changes," Monty said. "Get everyone out of that sphere as soon as possible."

"We're working on it," Roxanne said. "Your assistance will be appreciated."

Roxanne ended the call.

I had swerved off the line to the Lincoln Tunnel and was headed across town before she hung up.

"How bad is it? Why would the wards activate? Who or what is the Black Orchid?"

"The Black Orchid is a special sect of battle mages, an elite force created during the war," Monty said, gripping the door handle. "It was a clandestine group. Disavowed. That sort of thing."

"Mage Navy Seals?" I half-chuckled, then realized he wasn't smiling. "Black Ops?"

He nodded.

"We were given the missions too risky, insane, or deadly for the regular forces," Monty answered. "Presently, they are the ones who deal with renegade mages and abuses of power. When a mage goes dark, the Orchid is notified and tasked with bringing them in or termination. It's usually both."

"A mage hit squad?"

"Closer to mage police now," Monty corrected. "They exist to deter mages from delving into the darker aspects of the power we wield."

"Seriously? You were part of this group?"

"Seriously," he said. "During the war, I led a small team. We were ambushed. Everyone in my group except for myself and Roxanne was killed...Uncle Dex managed to get us out in time...barely."

"You think fake Fate is part of this dead group?"

"The wards around Haven are keyed to a group of specific energy signatures," Monty said. "It could be as Roxanne said, something else entirely. A false alarm."

"But you don't think so."

"The energy signature from Fate earlier today was familiar...I just can't place it."

"In the meantime—"

"Haven, Roxanne, is under attack," Monty said, flexing the muscles of his jaw. "Can we go faster?"

"I don't think Cecil installed a hyperdrive, but the Dark Goat can burn road when needed," I said as I stepped on the gas. "I'm guessing teleportation is out of the question?"

Things had to be desperate if I was suggesting the digestive destruction of teleportation, but I had never seen Monty this concerned.

"It would be pointless and dangerous," he said. "The wards and the sphere would react to any teleportation circle in their vicinity."

"What are the wards she was talking about?" I asked. "Who is after her?"

"There is an entropic sphere around the facility," Monty said, "specifically around the supernatural side."

"Roxanne said it's inert."

"Thankfully," Monty said, rubbing his face. "If it were active, our options would be limited. Teleporting through an active entropic sphere would be...difficult."

"How hard would it be?" I asked, speeding across town on 34th Street. "If Haven's under attack, we should get there right now."

"We can't," Monty said. "I doubt even my uncle could manage it, although he is mad enough to try. The qualities of the sphere would cancel out the cast, killing the caster. Even while it's inert. This is no ordinary cast."

"Whoa, this is some serious shit."

Monty nodded.

"An active entropic sphere is lethal," Monty said. "I haven't heard of their use since the war."

"Are you sure they're after Roxanne?" I asked, hoping against hope. "Maybe someone is just pissed at Haven? Didn't like their stay there and didn't want to submit a complaint to HR...Bam! Unleash an entropic circle, problem solved."

"This world of yours, the one where your brain roams freely, must truly be a fascinating place," Monty answered, staring at me. "Entropic spheres are not quite that easy to unleash. They are intricate and time consuming. Whoever did this, knows what they're doing. The target is Haven and Roxanne."

"Why?" I asked. "Why is Roxanne a target?"

"The fact that it's a sphere and the wards have activated, narrows it down somewhat," Monty said, after a moment of silence. "I may have an idea of who visited us this morning."

"Do I want to know?"

"Not really, but I'll tell you anyway. E-spheres, as they were called during the war, were horrible things. Mages on both sides used them before they were mutually outlawed."

"That bad?"

"Beyond," Monty answered, looking off into the distance. "They were created to dissolve living tissue. Mages would cast them around enemy positions and set them to slowly implode."

"Fuck, that's wrong."

"So is war," Monty said. "Doesn't stop us from killing each other."

"I just meant..."

"I know."

"Did you ever...?"

"Mages on *both* sides, Simon," Monty answered, his voice harder than steel. "Yes, I was ordered to cast one and only one. It was enough to last me a lifetime, several lifetimes. We called them Devourers. The e-spheres weren't soundproof or fast."

I shook my head at the imagery.

"The screams must've been..."

"The screams lasted days, as the trapped mages slowly died. It's a sound you never forget. The spheres were horrific."

"Horrific describes war well. How long did they—?"

"Not long. After the first casualties both sides agreed their use had crossed too many lines."

"Even war has rules."

"Indeed. Once the spheres were banned, we found more humane and efficient ways to kill each other," Monty said. "I thought the casting of the spheres lost, forgotten."

"Apparently someone remembered," I said. "Someone who was in the war."

"Someone strong enough to cast an entropic sphere, or at least have access to the information from the war...classified information."

"That can't be a large group," I said. "How many of the mages from that time are still around?"

"Impossible to say," Monty said. "It's not like they took a census. Many who survived went into hiding, changing identities, losing themselves to history."

"Is there any way to stop one of these Devourer spheres?"

"Yes, and it's as unpleasant as the sphere itself," Monty said, his jaw set. "Whoever did this is at least as old, if not older than I am, and practiced in forbidden mage warfare."

"Someone ancient, powerful, and angry. That just about describes everyone who doesn't like us."

"This is no easy cast."

"Fate managed to bypass all our security without a sweat. I've only seen Hades do something like that."

Monty nodded.

"Bypassing our defenses would require enormous amounts of energy and skill."

"Fate felt like she had the firepower. Maybe not Hades level, but she's no slouch."

"Perhaps," Monty answered, semi-lost in his thoughts. "I'd have to face her again to ascertain her true level."

"What's the counter to the sphere?" I asked. "How bad is it?"

"Bad enough to have the cast banned during a time of war," Monty said. "Bad enough to rob you of sleep for decades."

"Shit," I said. "What is it?"

"The counter requires knowledge of ancient magic, dark magic."

"Blood magic?" I asked, hoping the answer was something else.

"Blood magic," Monty said. "Usually lethal."

TWENTY

"There has to be another way," I said. "Blood magic can get you killed. It's too dangerous."

"You understand that Roxanne is in danger? Haven is *inside* one of these things?" Monty said. "Would you be looking for an alternative if it was Michiko? Or Peaches...or me?"

"Fuck!" I said, pounding the steering wheel. "There has to be another way."

"There isn't," Monty said, quietly. "If there were, don't you think I or Roxanne would know of it?"

"Call Dex," I said suddenly. "Maybe LD or TK can help? We don't have to do this alone."

"Calling them would only put them in danger," Monty said. "This is a message as much as it is a threat."

"A message? A message from whom?"

"Whoever cast this sphere is telling me that someone from my time in the Black Orchid is still present," Monty said. "Someone willing to use forbidden magic to attack a hospital full of defenseless people. There are other casts worse than a sphere. What do you think they would do if we got LD, TK, or my uncle involved?"

"I didn't think about that," I said. "Somehow I don't think we have enough firepower to deal with whoever did this."

"I know this is connected to our guest this morning," Monty said. "Her masking ability was formidable."

"Maybe they aren't connected?" I said. "Could it be this is all a coincidence?"

"Everything is connected, Simon. Why did our guest this morning want you to face Kali?"

"You mean besides trying to get me dead?" I asked. "My best guess is to get me out of the way...divide and conquer. That's what I would do."

"She used fear and intimidation to make you think you were culpable for the imbalance around you," Monty said. "She knew threatening those close to you would act as a catalyst."

"It worked," I said. "You threaten me, I'll take you seriously. You threaten my family? I'll raze the earth to stop you."

"Precisely. She knew exactly what to say and where to apply pressure."

"No kidding," I said. "That means she's been doing her homework on both of us. That was the reason for her visit. She needed to get me in motion, but why?"

"The express purpose was to have you reverse your curse," Monty said. "The pieces are there...I'm just not seeing how they fit, yet."

"More than that, if I'm mortal, you don't have backup," I said, thinking out loud. "If I were coming back to take you out because of some vendetta, I would try to remove any support system you had, especially the immortal kind. Make you vulnerable. Keep you alone."

"I'm a fairly accomplished mage," Monty answered. "Not to diminish your considerable skill, but I'm not exactly what you would call vulnerable."

"True, you may not be vulnerable," I said. "But without me, you'd be facing whoever this is alone. It could be they're counting on your unique brand of Montague stubbornness."

"That would mean I'm predictable," Monty snapped. "I am *not* predictable. What I am is..."

"In need of a hot cuppa right about now, yes?"

"Lucky guess," Monty huffed. "That proves nothing."

"Good thing you aren't predictable then," I said. "Like I said, she did her homework on *both* of us. What side of Haven is this junction Roxanne mentioned on?"

"The main junctions are between the two wings," Monty said. "The underground junctions are not accessible to the public."

"How many junctions are there?"

"There are four main passages between the normal and supernatural wings of Haven. Two of them above ground and two below, with one final independent passage leading directly from the supernatural wing to the detention level underground."

"Which one would Roxanne pick?" I asked. "Above or below?"

"Something like this? She'll be on the lower skywalk, just above ground level to evacuate everyone possible, while locking down the detention area. The wards keep the wings compartmentalized and locked down in case of a breach."

"Which means once they activate she would call you to meet at this specific junction?" I asked. "Not at one of the others?"

"The lower junction is the most practical and easiest to access," Monty answered. "The others are impractical during an emergency, with the lowest underground one being the most dangerous."

"That makes the one above ground-level the obvious choice. How safe is it?"

"It's a hardened neutral location and standard protocol meeting site," Monty said. "I would say fairly safe."

"The Randy Rump is supposed to be fairly safe as far as neutral locations go," I pointed out. "How many times have you detonated that 'safe' place?"

"Each time, I was reacting to an attack," Monty said. "But you make a fair point. We have to assume the junction isn't as secure as possible."

"You meet there to do what, exactly?"

"We meet at the junction to assess the damage and danger to Haven," Monty said. "From there we take the appropriate actions to deal with the threat. Think of it as an impromptu base of operations."

"Is the junction warded?" I asked, seeing the flaw. "Are there wards on the junction?"

"No, the junction is a null area between the wings. The wards would be ineffective in the junction. It possesses its own set of runic failsafes that make it a null zone."

"A null zone which would neutralize most of your abilities?"

"Mine and anyone else's. It's how they're designed."

"Could you cast on the junction?" I asked. "Not a theoretical mage, you personally."

"Not without tapping into dark magic," Monty answered. "There are workarounds to normal casting. Most involve blood magic."

"So, in order to cast on the junction, you have to use dangerous blood magic."

"I just said that."

"I'm thinking," I said. The pieces were almost fitting together but I still had gaps. "How strong are the failsafes on the junction?"

"The failsafes on the junctions are powerful," Monty said. "Only the most basic casts are allowed on them. The nullifying runes employed were designed to prevent major casting of any kind."

"Makes sense, considering the detention area is located on the premises. This means no serious casting on the skywalk, unless blood magic is used."

"Yes, but the junction itself is a protected area, like a bubble of power," Monty added. "Even blood magic would be dangerous and potentially lethal to the caster."

"Okay, let me see if I understand: the wards are activated, Roxanne calls you," I said, running down the sequence in my head. "Then you meet at the junction, the one just above ground level to assess the damage and danger, as standard protocol dictates. That about right?"

"So far, yes," Monty said. "Those are the recent emergency contingency protocols. Designed to protect Haven and its inhabitants, while keeping the detained confined to the detention level."

"Recent?" I asked. "How recent?"

"Ever since we started paying Haven regular visits."

"Oh," I said. "What was the protocol before it was changed?

"Compartmentalization, containment, and control," Monty said. "Both wings operate independently and the detention area is closed off."

"What changed?"

"Centralized coordination instead of a fragmented response. Roxanne handles damage control with redundant personnel in place and gets help from me."

"Who else knows of these protocols?"

"Besides the Directors, I'm sure most of the support personnel," Monty said. "This is general information to protect the integrity of the entire facility. It's drilled at regular intervals, at least once a month. As per Roxanne's instructions."

"It's SOP—standard operating procedure, which means predictable," I said. "Someone has been studying Roxanne, Haven, you, and the emergency protocols. If you go to the right junction, I can guarantee you won't leave it in one piece."

"Roxanne is heading there now," Monty said, urgency lacing his words as he grabbed his phone. We screeched to a stop as we pulled up in front of Haven. "I have to warn her."

We jumped out of the Dark Goat and headed inside. Peaches kept pace in tear-and-shred mode as people ran around us. Haven personnel were funneling people to different areas. Those who were too sick to move on their own were being assisted to safe locations.

"This is not a drill," I said, looking around at the activity. "There is a real threat here. Where is the sphere?"

"I need to find Roxanne. The energy signature from this morning...Fate's been here," Monty said. "The sphere would be on the other side of Haven. This is the normal side."

"Tell Roxanne to go underground," I said. "Use another junction, and secure the detention area with extra personnel. This whole thing feels like a distraction."

"A distraction?" Monty asked. "Distraction from what?"

"Let's say you had to face a powerful mage and needed some willing, readymade allies to take down said mage," I said, moving fast through Haven's lobby. "Where would you start looking for help?"

It took him a few seconds, but he finally connected the dots.

"Bloody hell," Monty hissed. "The detention area. The transplants from Sheol."

"Kind of convenient, don't you think? They're scheduled to be transferred in a week. Sounds familiar?"

"The deadline Fate gave you."

"Exactly," I said, nodding. "Keep us busy for a week, she gets an instamob, some of which actually dislike *you*. Imagine that."

"The plan must have changed somewhere," Monty said. "She acted prematurely."

"I'd say the recent turn of events may have something to do with that," I said. "It's possible she didn't expect this response. How many ways to get to the detention level?"

"Several, as you know: the elevator, the direct passage, and one external tunnel that's been sealed due to being a risk of escape."

"Let me guess, aside from the sealed tunnel, these are all in the supernatural wing?"

"Of course," Monty said, frustrated. "What sense would it make to have the access in the normal wing?"

"None," I said. "You're right."

"She won't pick up," Monty said, placing the phone in a pocket "I'm going to go find her."

"*We're* going to find her," I said, looking down at Peaches and holding up a finger. "Give me a second."

<Boy, I need you to find Roxanne, Monty's scary lady. Can you find her?>

Peaches sniffed the air for a few seconds before chuffing.

<I know where she is. She is up. Do you want to go to her?>

<Yes. Can you take Monty and me to where she is?>

<I can take you close. There are empty places here I can't see.>

I assumed he meant the junctions or wards were preventing him from going in-between.

<Take us as close as you can.> I grabbed Monty by the arm. *<Go. Now!>*

Haven tilted to one side and we slipped in-between. After what felt to me like a few seconds, we arrived several floors above our original location. My stomach was still en route, probably due to the suddenness of the shift.

The junction level was organized chaos.

There was more activity on this level. People were running back and forth, some with patients, others without. Everyone seemed to know where to go and what to do.

Klaxons were going off, together with a low humming sound and metal screeching. It sounded as if Haven was tearing itself apart. I saw Roxanne at the end of the corridor. She was still on the supernatural side of Haven. Based on her expression and hand motions, she was giving several people directions on what to do and where to go.

Behind her, I could see the shimmering effect of the sphere. It pulsed slowly with a dim violet light, refracting everything that was inside of it. I realized after a few seconds that the sphere was the source of the low humming.

"Monty, over there," I said, pointing. "Across the junction."

"Bloody hell, the whole junction is compromised," he said, looking down the skywalk. "What is she doing? The entire structure is volatile."

The junction was an enclosed skywalk between the two wings, talk about bad planning. I'm sure someone thought this looked amazing and avant-garde. I just saw a death trap with a view. Whoever designed these skywalks didn't stop to think they were excellent choke points and easily attacked.

Roxanne turned in our direction and caught sight of Monty. She started moving fast toward us. I raised a hand, yelling for her to stop, but it was futile, my voice was drowned out by the noise.

She closed the distance and I felt the energy surge before I saw anything. I turned just in time to see Monty run forward, gesturing on the way, his hands covered in dark red and black energy.

Peaches growled and backed up fast.

<It smells bad. The angry man is going to the bad smell.>

<He's going to help Roxanne. We need to get away. That energy is dangerous.>

I shifted to move away from the edge of the junction. That's when I noticed the wards on its surface. They gradually went from barely visible to blinding white, forcing me to shield my eyes.

<The angry man needs help. I will go help him so he can make extra meat.>

<No! That's a bad idea, boy. Move back!>

Before I could grab him, Peaches ran between my legs toward Monty and Roxanne. His dash knocked me off balance, forcing me to rotate my body to stay on my feet. I saw Monty reach Roxanne, as a large orb of violet and black energy surged in the center of the skywalk, obscuring my view. I jumped back as it expanded, blowing the skywalk apart with a deafening explosion.

TWENTY-ONE

The ringing in my ears was a constant high trill as I regained consciousness. The smell of charred metal and plastic assaulted my nostrils as I struggled to see through the smoke of what was left of the skywalk.

"That...was not fun," I said with a groan, as I shifted metal and debris away from my body. "Ouch, you'd think by now I'd be used to these sorts of explosions. Totally didn't see that one coming."

I took a moment to assess the damage to Haven, the skywalk, and my body. The center of the skywalk was a gaping hole, as if a giant had punched a fist through it. Parts of the junction swayed, while other sections fell several dozen feet down to the street.

I could hear sirens in the distance from the first responders. They were going to have their hands full dealing with this mess. I looked around for Peaches, Monty, Roxanne...anyone. The junction area was deserted. I staggered to my feet and leaned against a wall. My body flushed hot as it dealt with the damage. This time it felt as if I had stepped into a forge.

"Peaches! Monty! Roxanne!" I yelled out. "Where are you?"

No response, except for the low humming. I looked across the junction and saw the sphere still pulsing. There was a minimal energy signature coming off it.

"Did we get blown into another dimension?" I muttered out loud, looking across the gap. "Wouldn't surprise me with the day I've been having."

<*Peaches? Where are you, boy?*>

The runes along the surface of the skywalk flickered with a dull orange light.

"So much for this place being a neutral zone. Someone set this up."

"You should have gone straight to Kali like I suggested," a familiar voice said from behind me. "She would have eliminated you and opened an easier path for me. Now *I* have to kill you."

Fate.

"No need to be hasty," I said, turning to face her. "I don't want you to have to exert yourself."

"Has anyone ever found you remotely funny?"

"Peaches finds me hilarious as long as there is meat to be had," I said. "Monty probably finds me mildly annoying."

"You're an irritant at best, one that needs to be removed."

"Who are you? Really?" I asked. "Don't give me this BS about you being Fate. We both know that's not true."

"True enough to get you motivated," Fate said. "You have served your purpose."

"My purpose?" I asked. "You don't even know me. How would you know my purpose?"

"I know you, Simon Strong, better than you can imagine."

"That was some performance this morning," I said, making sure Grim Whisper was still in its holster. "Who, what are you?"

"The result of Tristan's betrayal," she answered. "I'm karma coming due."

"Trust me, you're not Karma," I said. "I've met her, and you're not even close. Wait...are you part of Black Orchid?"

She cocked her head to one side with a smile. A decidedly 'I'm not in my right mind' sort of smile, just this side of psychopathic. An acrid smell permeated the corridor. It was a mix of burnt copper and flesh, causing me to nearly lose my pastrami sandwich.

"He told you?"

"He may have mentioned something about a special group, and all of them dying in the war," I answered. "If you're not Fate, then you are...?"

"Evers, second in command of the original Black Orchid after the traitor, Montague," she said. "The true Black Orchid, not the watered down version of glorified mage police that exists today. We were the first. Swift, lethal, and unseen. In my day, just the mention of our presence would send mages running in a panic."

"What? The BO did not believe in deodorant back then?" I asked. "That would certainly qualify as swift, lethal, and unseen. In fact,"—I covered my face with a hand—"I think you may still need to work on the freshness. Is that smell you?"

Evers narrowed her eyes at me. She maintained her composure better than most, but I knew I had pushed some buttons.

"That delicious smell," she said with a sniff of the air, "is the death of Tristan Montague."

"You're strong," I said, ignoring her comment. "How did you mask your signature so completely?"

"Practice."

"How did you know about Kali and me? The curse?"

"The Chosen of Kali," Evers mocked. "I'm older than Tristan. Once I heard about the destructive detective agency in this city, one a mage and the other an immortal, it was a simple matter of research...I knew where to look and who to ask."

"Who did you ask?"

"A better question is: who would want to see your so-called detective agency destroyed?"

"Listen, I don't want to hurt you, but it's still on my list, right after you answer the question. Who?"

She laughed. It was a low guttural sound that pinged all of my fight or flight responses...heavy on the flight.

"I wouldn't worry about it, Chosen One," Evers said. "Nothing good was said."

"You can't believe everything you hear, you know," I said, glancing around and realizing I was still alone. "Most of them are just jealous of my skills."

"Skills?" Evers scoffed. "You may be immortal but you are just a babe."

"I know I'm hard to resist, but I'm in a serious relationship with a—never mind," I said, shaking my head. "Would take too long to explain. Let's just say I've met my quota on psychopathic women for the rest of my unnatural life. Thanks for the offer, but no thanks."

"I'm going to make sure you and Tristan suffer before I end you both."

She was still in seething mode, and I needed her to explode—maybe make a mistake I could exploit. It was either that or be painfully blown to bits. If I could get her angry, I could get her to show her hand and hopefully slip up.

It was time for diplomacy.

"What you said about my affecting causality and restoring balance...another lie?"

"No, you were how I found Montague," she answered with a laugh. "Your scattered energy signature is easy to read, if one knows where to look. You *will* help me restore balance, once Tristan's dead body lies at my feet."

"And he talks about the women in my life...wow," I said. "I'm afraid I'm going to have to cancel the death of Monty."

"You still don't understand," she answered before sharing more of her psycho laugh. "He's already dead, he just doesn't know it yet. He had to use blood magic to get his woman safe. That sealed his end."

"What are you talking about?"

"I'm not here for you. I'm here for the others," Evers said, gathering energy around her. "You just happen to be in the way. You, I'm going to kill you for fun."

"You and I have very different ideas about fun. Wait, others?" I asked. "What others?"

Evers pointed a finger down, and then it started to make sense.

"Monty said you were all gone," I paraphrased. "Something to the effect of you all got wiped out."

"Some of us survived. Not all of us were killed."

"Be honest, was it because of you?"

"Because of me?" Evers said, raising her voice. "It was Montague that led us into that trap. He killed us. He is the reason I lost...everything."

"You seem pretty alive," I said. "How exactly did he kill you?"

"Because of him, my ability to cast was erased. Because of him, I had to take...measures...to regain my power. You, of all people, must realize that there are worse things than physical death."

"Talk about holding a grudge," I said, backing up and away from the skywalk. If she was going to get mage conversational, I didn't want my back to a gaping hole. "This happened how long ago? You're still pissed? I mean what could you have possibly lost that was so important? I mean, besides your mind."

"You know, before, it was going to be a chore to dispatch you," she said, not making any attempt to hide her energy signature anymore. It was immense. "Now, I'm going to enjoy blasting you to atoms. Not even Kali's curse will help you this time."

I felt the tingle of an energy signature down the back of my neck and I changed direction, heading back to the skywalk. There was no way I could take her on alone, or even with a small army. I was going to need to be evasive. In other words, I needed to run away.

"I don't need a curse to deal with an amateur like you," I said, stepping onto the skywalk. I felt it sway under my weight as a piece of railing fell off and crashed to the ground. "In fact, I don't need anyone to finish you off."

"You are a stupid man," Evers said, forming a wicked-looking silver-black orb of energy. "A dead stupid man."

She released the orb and sent it racing in my direction.

TWENTY-TWO

Several things happened in that moment.

The voice in my head, which had by now grown accustomed to the near-death experiences of my past, had long since stopped screaming at me. It merely peered at the incoming orb and advised me to not get hit if I wanted to continue to remain among the breathing.

Sage advice.

At that same moment, the skywalk started to give beneath me causing me to backpedaled and lose my balance. This was all framed in the context of Evers laughing as she walked away, certain that her orb of death would erase me from existence.

The tingle I felt earlier grew stronger, as I pinwheeled my arms and fell backwards into the gap. Evers' orb of destruction followed me down. I glanced over my shoulder, and realized I was a good thirty feet from the concrete below.

They didn't call my city the concrete jungle for nothing. If I made it to the ground below, that concrete was going to reach up and introduce me to a world of pain. It would still probably hurt less than the angry looking orb that was chasing me down.

As I fell, and contemplated death by orb or by concrete, I felt a sharp pain in my side, and the world melted away into darkness.

When I could see again, I realized I was in a dark, underground corridor with a hellhound attached to my waist. Focusing, as my eyes adjusted to the darkness, I saw Roxanne and a prone Monty laying on the ground.

<*You can stop biting me now, boy. I'm glad to see you too.*>

<*The scary lady said to bring you. The angry man is sick.*>

<*She spoke to you? The same way I do?*>

<*No. She is not my bondmate but she said: 'get Simon', so I brought you here.*>

<*Thanks for getting me, but what took so long?*>

<*The angry man made some angry energy and I got lost. I found him and the scary lady. He was sick. Then she said to get you. It didn't take long.*>

<*Did you try using your saliva on him?*>

<*I did. He is too sick. My saliva is excellent, but I don't think it's strong enough for his sickness.*>

I slowly stood up, making sure the floor didn't tilt away from my feet as I stumbled over to where Roxanne knelt. She was casting dark red energy over Monty's body.

"What's wrong with him?" I asked as the smell from the skywalk wafted up to my nose. "Oh, no. Side effects of the blood magic?"

"He saved me," Roxanne said, her voice choking up. "The stupid fool cast blood magic as the wards exploded."

"She knew he would," I almost whispered. "She knew he would save you by sacrificing himself."

"What are you talking about? Who knew that?"

"Evers, the woman who posed as Fate in our office this morning."

"What did you say her name was?"

"Evers. Short black hair, silver glasses, black power suit, extra dose of energy with a dash of psycho?"

"Bloody hell," Roxanne said, looking down at Monty. "He was right. Evers was the second-in-command of the original Black Orchid. What could she possibly want?"

"Looks like she's still pissed at Monty for some situation during his Orchid days," I said. "Basically she wants him dead."

"She may have gotten what she wants," Roxanne said. "He's in critical condition."

"That's not all she wants," I said. "She's here for those detainees you had to relocate into the lower levels. Can we stop her?"

"Not from here," Roxanne said. "Haven Detention is under the supernatural wing. These are the subbasements to the normal wing."

"The junction to the supernatural wing?"

"Is inside the sphere," Roxanne answered. "If we try anything, and she makes it active, I don't think even you would survive. That sphere is a Devourer."

"Monty shared. Nasty sphere of death," I said, shaking my head. "The first priority is getting him better."

"I'm afraid I can't improve his condition," Roxanne said. "The damage is too extensive. He used blood magic that was beyond even me. The most I can do is protect him by placing his body in stasis."

"How bad is it?"

Roxanne looked away while Peaches whined and put his head down.

"If we don't reverse the cast, he will schism," she said, her voice hard. "Then he will die."

"Schism?" I asked, not following. "What does that mean?"

"It means he will become dark, consumed by the blood magic, and then ultimately destroyed. The Tristan you and I know would cease to exist. He would transform into a twisted, dark mage, with phenomenal power."

"Like Evers."

Roxanne nodded.

"Worse, because he has more potential than she does," Roxanne said. "He would become stronger, even more powerful than Evers. Stronger than any mage you know, even Dex."

"Potential," I repeated. "You said he has potential. That's what he told me. He told me I had potential to become a powerful mage."

Roxanne shook her head with a look of sadness.

"That would take years, Simon, decades. He doesn't have that kind of time."

"Who could reverse this?" I asked, angry and frustrated. "Who has the power we need?"

"You need an astronomical amount of power to undo this cast," Roxanne said as her eyes began to tear. "Beyond Archmage level. You would need power approximating..."

"A god?"

"Do you know how to get in contact with Hades?" Roxanne asked, hope in every word. "Maybe your hellhound can locate him?"

"I don't think that would work," I said, and watched

her expression sink into despair. “Once, he told me the bonds only work with a particular hellhound. Hades is bound to Cerberus.”

“Then I’ll reach out to Julien or Honor, one of them will help Tristan,” she said, determined. “I will make sure of it.”

“You just said we need beyond-Archmage-level of power,” I said gently. “I know Julien is powerful, I can’t speak for this Honor person, but I think I know someone who can help.”

“Who?” Roxanne asked, all her hope placed in one word. “You know a god who can help?”

“No, but I know a goddess.”

TWENTY-THREE

"You're insane," Roxanne said, staring at me. "Kali will kill you the moment you set foot in her temple, if you even make it to her temple alive."

"It's Monty," I said, looking down. "Do you have a better option?"

"No one wants him to recover as much as I do," she shot back. "Don't you dare question my concern."

"Sorry."

"You should be," she said and softened her voice. "He wouldn't want you to throw your life away in the process. That goddess is dangerous. She's not known as Kali the Destroyer because she's merely cranky. Visiting her is beyond foolish. She is volatile on a good day."

"I'm not hearing an alternative here," I said. "Kali can also deal with what's going on with my energy signature."

"Your energy signature?"

"Is out of whack," I said. "Can't you tell?"

"Have my hands full...literally," she said, looking down at Monty. "But your signature does seem off. What is it?"

"Monty said something about affecting causality, then he lost me," I said. "That's why I need to go see Kali."

"You figured you'd pop in and do one of those 'I just happened to be in the neighborhood' moments with her?" Roxanne asked, staring at me. "She...will...kill...you. Am I not being clear?"

"Crystal," I said, looking at the black energy around Monty. "Regardless, I'm his shieldbearer, and right now he needs me to get to her."

"Certainly," Roxanne mocked. "I'll just pull up her address. Give me a moment."

"Well, I can see what Monty sees in you," I answered. "You two have the identical sense of humor...none. I'm not asking you to come with; I just need a little help getting there."

"Should I flag you a taxi?" she deadpanned. "I'm sure Cecil makes a SuNaTran extra-planar edition. Perhaps we can reach out to him?"

Anyone else and I would've had a comeback ready, but occasionally my sense of self-preservation kicks in and reminds me of just who I'm facing. Roxanne was a powerful sorceress who was kneeling over a person she cared deeply about.

In the midst of this, the facility she was responsible for was under attack. I'd say she was handling it pretty well. There was no need for me to upset her further with one of my comments. I'm sensitive that way.

"Good one," I said, keeping my voice serious. "No need to escort us, just get us to the door...in one piece if possible."

"I couldn't leave Haven now even if I wanted to," Roxanne said, looking behind her. "That entropic sphere endangers everyone, and, if you're right, I need to reinforce the lower levels of the detention area with more security."

"Don't forget the sealed tunnel," I reminded her. "That's what I would use if I were Evers. Guaranteed to be overlooked."

"Bloody hell," she muttered. "I completely forgot about the tunnel. It's been sealed for so long, it wasn't even a consideration."

"Which is why she will use it."

"How did *you* know about it?"

"Monty mentioned it before everything went Montague-shaped," I said, glancing at Monty. "He does have a tendency to be explosive."

"Frankly," Roxanne answered with a rueful smile, "I really don't know how you two have survived this long."

"We've turned it into an art form."

"Surviving or the destruction of your immediate surroundings?"

"Both?" I said. "This Evers is bad news. She's strong, smart, and sprinkled with ample doses of batshittiness. She nearly hit me with one of her orbs."

"Silver-black orb with nastiness written all over it?"

"The one and the same. Felt like getting hit by it would make for a bad day."

"Listen to me carefully, Simon," Roxanne said, measuring her words. "Under no circumstance should you allow one of those orbs to hit you. Do you understand?"

"That bad?"

"Whatever you're imagining, it's worse. Evers is a chronomancer. Those orbs she uses create a pocket of frozen time and then accelerate your aging in mere seconds. They *will* kill you."

"Avoid crazy chronomancer with killer orbs...check," I answered. "Can you make it so Monty can travel?"

"In that death trap you call a vehicle? Impossible. The runes Cecil used in your death machine would wreak havoc with the stasis field I would need to place around him."

"Would a normal teleport impact the stasis field?"

Roxanne paused in thought before answering.

"A normal teleport to where? Kali isn't even on this plane, Simon."

"We need to go to Jersey."

"You're telling me Kali the Destroyer is living somewhere in New Jersey? What, she vacations at the shore? The notion is preposterous."

"I need to get to Jersey," I said. "I never said Kali *lived* there."

"Mmhmm," Roxanne said with a nod, as she narrowed her eyes at me. "How close were you to the skywalk when it exploded?"

"I was on it, but that's not what I meant."

"Of course not," she said, nodding and slipping into triage mode. "How much debris impacted your head? I'll see what I can do. Do you feel dizzy? How's your vision? How many hellhounds"—she pointed at Peaches with her chin—"do you see sitting over there?"

"Stop it," I snapped. "I'm fine. Kali isn't *in* Jersey."

"Obviously," Roxanne agreed. "I've been saying that for the last five minutes."

"You didn't let me finish. She isn't there, but the door to her is in Jersey," I replied. "According to my sources, the door to Kali's domain is thinner at certain locations. The temple in Jersey will lead me to one of the doors."

"Your sources? Since when do you have *sources*? How do you know you can trust these 'sources' of yours? You thought Evers was Fate. Forgive me if I'm not entirely convinced by your powers of observation."

"Hey, no fair," I said. "I've never met Evers, or Fate. How was I supposed to be able to tell them apart?"

"Fate," Roxanne said, her voice on edge, "would never come to you *or* Tristan for help. That should have been the first and most obvious indicator, but your immortal ego and Tristan's insufferable curiosity couldn't see past the truth staring you both in the face."

"Which truth?"

"Simon, nothing is 'fated' in our lives. You, of all people should know that, you're a living example of it. Tristan as well. We make choices, and we accept and deal with the repercussions of those choices, good or bad."

"I do know this. That's why I need to get to Jersey."

"You mean to tell me that in this temple, there is a portal that will lead to Kali the Destroyer?" Roxanne asked. "That isn't how access to gods works, Simon."

"Haven't I been clear?"

"Absolutely," Roxanne said, shaking her head and refocusing on Monty. "Clearly out of your mind."

"Mori, Death's—capital D—PA gave me this information."

"Gods don't just have portals where just anyone can access them, Simon. It's a difficult process usually..."

"Really? So, Hades having an office in downtown Manhattan isn't how access to gods works?"

"Well, that's a peculiar instance of..."

"Dex dating The Morrigan, the Chooser of the Slain, is just a run-of-the-mill relationship...right?"

"No, that's quite odd actually..."

"The fact that Ezra is also Azrael the Angel of Death, and has a deli where he hangs out is also the norm. In addition to facing Tartarus and Chaos, two of the old gods, I'd say I have more experience with how access to gods works than you do."

"You don't, but you've made your point," Roxanne said. "I must say, you have encountered some incredible beings during your cases. It makes sense now, the level of destruction and havoc you have wreaked in this city."

"*I* have wreaked?" I asked incredulously and pointed at Monty. "What about your mage boyfriend?"

"I didn't say he was blameless," Roxanne answered. "Together,"—she glanced at Peaches—"you three are a clear and present danger to this city, but we need you to stand against the greater threats we face."

"The disease is worse than the remedy? Thanks, I think."

"I wouldn't go that far, but you come close," Roxanne replied, raising her hands away from Monty. "There, he's stabilized for now. When he regains consciousness, under no circumstances can you allow him to cast."

"What happens?" I asked, actually scared. "Does he explode? Should I not feed him after midnight?"

Roxanne stared at me for a few seconds before shaking her head.

"If he casts, he will accelerate the schism," Roxanne said, her voice grim. "He cast blood magic without releasing the reagent first. If you make it to Kali alive, she will know what to do...or she will obliterate you both.

Depends on her mood when she sees you. It may be best to try tact and diplomacy first."

"Not my strong points, but okay."

"If you don't, I'm pretty certain she will blast you to dust," Roxanne said. "I'd suggest you try your best."

"That's comforting, really."

"I'm not here to comfort you, Simon," she said. "I'm prepared to lose Tristan every time the two of you face-off against some threat to the city. He's come close a few times, but this time...this time I don't know."

"I'll do everything possible to bring him back in one piece," I said. "He's tougher than he looks."

"I know," she said and began gesturing. A few seconds later a large, red, teleportation circle formed under Monty. I looked down at it warily, not entirely sure if it was safe. "That should take you where you need to go."

"How did you even know how to form the circle?" I asked. "It's not like I gave you an address."

"Simple," Roxanne said. "I merely entwined the basic strands of your energy signature—even in its altered chaotic state, it has traces of Kali. Haven't you ever wondered how people know you are the 'Chosen of Kali'?"

"They can see it in my signature?"

"Yes," Roxanne said with a brief nod. "She basically painted a bullseye on you. I'd say she was upset when she chose you."

"You think?" I said, examining the runes in the teleportation circle. "So, this circle will lead me to the Jersey temple?"

"It should," Roxanne answered. "It will lead you to the greatest concentration of energy that matches the undercurrent in your own signature. I would assume that is the temple in Jersey if it is connected to Kali. Unless she has another temple close by?"

"That's the only one I know that leads to her," I said, still looking down at the circle. "What happens if you're wrong?"

"I'm not a teleportation master, like Dex, but my skills are above par," she answered. "I wouldn't risk Tristan's life or yours recklessly. If I'm wrong, grab your hellhound and find your way there or back to Haven."

"Either way, we can't stay here," I said, stepping into the circle. "I really hope she's in a good mood."

"It's not just her you need to worry about," Roxanne added, as the circle began to glow and slowly rotate. "She employs dozens of Rakshasas as her personal guard. Try not to anger them. Do you have a way to access the portal once you're in the temple?"

I looked down at the mark on my hand.

"I have an idea," I said. "If that doesn't work, this trip is over before it began."

"I hope it works," Roxanne said, gesturing again. "Take care of him, Simon."

"I will. Is this teleportation going to be uncomfortable? You know I'm not a fan of these circles."

Peaches padded over and stood next to Monty.

"It shouldn't be too excruciating," she said with a slight smile, rubbing Peaches' head. She crouched and whispered something into his ear, before standing again. "It will feel like your insides are trying to escape your body, but nothing too bad."

"Nothing too bad?"

"Bring him back to me whole, Shieldbearer."

"I will," I said, meaning it. "I'll make sure he gets better."

She nodded, gesturing again and forcing the circle to blaze with red light, blinding me.

With a lurch, we shifted away from Haven.

TWENTY-FOUR

The smooth marble felt cool against my cheek as my hellhound proceeded to nuzzle his face into my own. Normally, this wouldn't be a problem, except hellhounds were notoriously slobbery creatures—at least this was my opinion from my limited experience with the species.

If I didn't move his head, I'd end up swimming across the floor. I placed a hand on his massive head and pushed, shoving myself across the marble and away from where he stood, immobile.

The afternoon sun was slowly fading from the skylights above me as night approached. I lay on the stairs leading to the entrance of an ornate, white marble temple. It was an odd feeling because the temple I was looking at sat inside a larger structure. A building inside of a building.

I had a brief Escheresque moment, as I looked around and saw several signs advising against photography beyond certain points or against touching the sculptures of the temple.

Another small plaque informed me that the temple I

currently inhabited was actually called a Mandir, and that presently I lay on the floor of the Baps Shri Swaminarayan Mandir, which had been consecrated by his Holiness Pramukh Swami Maharaj, on a hot August day.

It was about to be defiled by yours truly as I felt my pastrami lunch travel upwards. I took several deep breaths, turned to lay on my back, and remained as still as possible as my stomach settled down. I would have hated to piss-off the good Swami by redecorating the Italian marble with pastrami vomit.

<*Should I lick you? You don't look good.*>

<*I don't feel good either. Teleportation doesn't agree with my body.*>

<*Because you don't eat enough meat. If you ate more meat you could go in-between without feeling sick.*>

<*If I ate meat, or anything for that matter, before teleporting, it would be a digestive mess on the other side of the teleport, trust me.*>

<*I still think I should lick you. The angry man is still sleeping.*>

<*That's...that's good. Give me a second while my body calms down.*>

<*My body never needs to calm down.*>

<*What did Roxanne tell you?*>

<*She said that if it gets very bad, to bring you and the angry man to her. No matter what.*>

<*How is it that you can understand her?*>

<*I'm the smartest hellhound you know. I can understand everyone.*>

<*You're the only hellhound I know.*>

<*Which makes me the smartest hellhound you know.*>

<*Your logic is astounding at times.*>

<I'm hungry.>

<Of course you are. I don't think I can get meat for you right now. Once Monty wakes up, I'll see if he can walk me through the cast.>

<You're going to make the meat?>

<If Monty shows me, it should be doable.>

<Can the angry man make it for me? I don't want you to break my stomach.>

<You said you were hungry.>

<I'm also smart. Eating meat you make is not smart, it hurts.>

<Then you will have to be patient. Can you wait?>

<I think so. You should practice making the meat so I can eat it.>

<Right, I'll get on that right away after we help Monty.>

I looked over and saw Monty still unconscious. I stood unsteadily and made my way over to where he lay. My body flushed warm as it dealt with the aftereffects of the teleport. So much for reconciling my bonds to make these instant trips easier. Clearly, I was destined to suffer through teleports.

Roxanne's words came back to me: *Simon, nothing is fated in our lives.*

This was one of those moments where we were going to agree to disagree. My stomach felt like it had been repeatedly tapped with a twenty pound sledgehammer. I groaned as I snaked my arms under Monty's armpits and half-carried, half-dragged him into the temple proper.

Monty was still covered in dark energy that enveloped his body like a tight cocoon. It almost felt repellant to my hands as I grabbed him. Like the same pole of two magnets trying to connect but sliding away from each other. It felt like he wanted to jump out of my arms as I adjusted my grip.

He stirred as we moved, but remained unconscious. For someone so thin, he was particularly dense, which made moving him an effort. It was like dragging a sandbag full of steel.

Thin but dense. The thought brought a smile to my face.

I sat on one of the white marble benches to catch my breath after pulling him into the center of the mandir. I looked around and took in the ornate marble. The stone work was exquisite, with carvings of elephants, goddesses, and intricate designs covering every inch of the temple.

The scope of the work was staggering to behold. As spectacular as the work was, I didn't notice a door that said 'This way to Kali's Domain', which meant I was going to have to try my method and hope it worked the way I expected.

Like that ever happened.

<I need you to watch over Monty, boy.>

<Where are you going? Are you going to get some meat?>

<I'm going to look for a door.>

<I see many doors. Are your eyes broken? There are doors over there.>

He stood at attention, doing his best arrow impersonation, pointing at several doors with his nose, followed by his entire body.

<Not those kinds of doors. I'm looking for a special kind of door. One that will take us somewhere to get help for Monty.>

<That is a good door. Will that door have meat?>

<I don't think so, but I'll make sure to double-check just for you.>

<Thank you, bondmate. I will guard the sick, angry man.>

<Thank you, boy.>

I stepped several feet away and sat cross-legged on the cool floor. I closed my eyes and steadied my breathing until I managed to get it completely under control. I let my senses expand, making sure I was alone, except for Peaches and Monty. After a few minutes, I was certain it was just us three in the temple.

I took one long breath, and slowly exhaled before reaching out and pressing the mark on my hand.

TWENTY-FIVE

The design, an endless knot inscribed into the top of my hand, given to me courtesy of Kali, gave off a golden light which increased in intensity until I had to look away.

"That's new," I muttered. "Usually the output is much lower than 'small sun bursting from my hand' level."

I looked around again and saw trails of light dancing in my vision.

Gradually, everything grew out of focus. The heady smell of lotus blossoms and earth after a hard rain filled my lungs. This was followed by the sharp smell of cut oranges and an aroma hinting of cinnamon permeating the air.

Time slowed and came to a pronounced and definitive standstill. I noticed the motes of dust suspended in the air as time crept to a visceral halt. This sensation was unlike the other times. This time, time took its time slowing down to the point of no time.

"Hello, Splinter," Karma said, sitting next to me. "This...is a nice change."

Karma looked around the area, taking in the temple. I glanced sidelong at her, keeping my distance just in case she wanted to share a slap hello. She wore a black Tom Ford Asymmetric One-Sleeve Bodycon Dress, which flattered her curves.

Her hair was down and considerably shorter than the last time I saw her. I noticed she wore only one earring, opposite the exposed arm. It was a small diamond 'B' that reflected the ambient light inside the mandir. She finished the ensemble with a pair of black Ferragamo Gancini pumps, sporting heels that were weapons in their own right.

"Dinner party tonight?" I asked, impressed by the clothing she wore. "Or are you dressed for an upscale funeral?"

"A little of both."

"Oh, I didn't know you had a social life," I said. "What with all the reaping and sowing business."

Karma narrowed her eyes at me and smiled, chilling my blood and making every hair on the back of my neck stand on end. I had the distinct feeling this was how a gazelle felt right before a lioness sprinted in for the kill.

"In fact, I have a few stops to make after we speak," Karma said, resting her hands on the knee of her crossed leg. "Did you learn the difference between Karma and Fate?"

"I thought I knew it," I said, answering carefully. I was still within arm's reach. "Seems my definition was slightly off."

"Enlighten me."

"Fate is something that's been pre-determined. Choice is removed from the equation."

"So far so good, continue."

"Karma"—I nodded in her direction—"is the result of my choices. The outcome of my actions."

"Where do you feel the definition lacks clarity?" Karma asked, looking over to where Monty lay on the floor. "That seems accurate."

"Except I fell for Evers' ruse when she pretended to be Fate. Even after you warned me."

"Because you chose to."

"I didn't choose to fall for the deception."

"You had the indicators before you, but you ignored them," she answered. "What choice are you making now?"

"I don't understand."

"Regarding your mage," Karma said, pointing to Monty. "What choice are you making now?"

"Monty is hurt," I said. "I need to help him."

"He made a choice," Karma replied, her voice soft. "This is his karma."

"What choice?" I asked, getting angry. "He was saving Roxanne. She would've been blown apart on the skywalk if he hadn't acted. He didn't have a choice."

"No. Wrong," Karma said. "He chose to use blood magic without first releasing the blood from his body. He chose to run to the sorceress, knowing full well the skywalk was a neutral area. This was not a series of 'accidents', Splinter. These were deliberate actions."

"What was he supposed to do? Let Roxanne get blown to bits?"

"I didn't say that," she said. "The same way your impact on causality is a result of the choices you have made. He lies here because of the choices he has made."

"I'm his shieldbearer, I need to help him."

"Do you?"

"What kind of question is that?"

"A simple one. All of our choices are linked, and interact with the choices others make. I'm not passing judgement. I am simply a mirror to your life."

"A 'you reap what you sow' sort of thing?" I asked. "Isn't that a bit cliche?"

"Like deeds lead to like effects," Karma said. "That is a simplification. The truth is deeper and more complex... like you. What choice are you making now?"

"I'm choosing to help Monty. To do that, I need your help."

"What if I refuse?"

"I'll have to find another way," I said. "It's not like I can make you help me...you have to choose to do so."

"Precisely," she said, as if I had uncovered some secret known to everyone but me. "The time will come when you will see the choice you've made."

"I hope by that time, I can understand half of what we just discussed."

"There may be hope for you yet, Splinter," Karma said with a nod. "The door you need is through that archway." She pointed straight ahead. "That will lead you to Kali's domain...and to your next choice."

My gaze followed her arm. She was pointing to a series of ornate, sequential arches that increased in size with each arch. The last arch was the most ornate, with decorations of a sword-bearing dancing goddess sculpted into the marble.

"Could I have found it without you?"

"That's not the real question, Splinter."

"Then what is the real question?" I asked, keeping my

frustration in check. I didn't forget that Karma was off-the-charts powerful, and that while time was in stasis...I was mortal. "Can you tell me the real question?"

"No, I cannot," she said, shaking her head. "That would only set you back."

"Not even a hint? I mean, really."

"I really enjoy our conversations, Splinter," she said, tapping me on the cheek and nearly dislocating my jaw. "They are...refreshing."

"I'm glad one of us is enjoying these conversations," I said, rubbing my face. "I usually leave them more confused than when we started."

"I will tell you one thing that can help," she said, standing. "The way to balance your signature is in your possession. Think inside the box."

"Right," I said, as time regained its normal flow. "That makes perfect sense."

Karma was gone.

TWENTY-SIX

"Where are we?" Monty asked as he came to. "Where's Roxanne? Who placed a stasis field around me?"

"Jersey, Haven, and Roxanne," I said. "She said you'll go schizo if you cast, so no wiggling of the fingers. If you try, I will be forced to break them."

"You realize that the hand gestures are not what power the casting?"

"Don't care," I said. "I see your fingers wiggling, I'm snapping them like twigs."

"It's 'schism' not schizo, by the way," he answered, standing unsteadily. "I underestimated the strength of the neutral area."

"You blew up the skywalk?" I asked.

"No," Monty answered. "It was the side effect of casting that sphere of protection around Roxanne. There were runes present that shouldn't have been there."

"Basically, what you're saying is that someone sabotaged the skywalk expecting you to cast on it?"

"Yes."

"And that in your sense of urgency, you cast to protect Roxanne?"

"Obviously, her safety was paramount."

"The sphere of protection you cast, interacted with the runes on the skywalk, causing a chain reaction which blew the neutral area to bits," I said. "That about right?"

"We've already been over this...yes."

"Then YOU blew up the skywalk...right?"

"Well, if you want to get technical about things, I suppose I had some small part to play in the disintegration of the neutral area," Monty said, waving my words away. "More importantly, how is Roxanne?"

"She's fine," I said, shaking my head. "Your sphere of protection transported you both several levels under Haven."

"We need to get back," Monty said. "Whoever cast that sphere is very likely still in the vicinity."

"Evers," I said. "That name ring a bell?"

"Bloody hell, that's impossible. I saw Evers die."

"Well, I don't know what you think you saw," I said. "I had a little chat with her as she was trying to melt me."

"You faced her?"

"Hell, no," I answered. "I ran away. She threw some silver-black orb at me. It gave off a serious 'I'm going to erase you painfully' vibe. I took a dive off the skywalk, and Peaches caught me...because he's a good boy."

I rubbed Peaches' massive head as he padded close.

<I think that deserves some meat. I saved you from bouncing on the street.>

<Would you like me to make some meat for you?>

<You?>

<I'm sure it will be better than last time.>

<Have you practiced?>

<You don't practice at being a hellhound. Why should I practice?>

<You aren't a mage like the angry man.>

<You make a good point. We'll have to wait.>

I just got outlogicized by my Zen Meatmaster hellhound.

"Evers is a chronomancer," Monty said. "If one of those orbs hit you..."

"Roxanne explained the killer orbs," I said. "Time stasis followed by time acceleration equals dead me."

"Not exactly the terminology I would use but yes, it would result in your demise. Or anyone's for that matter," Monty said, looking around. "Why are we here?"

"You screwed up something when you blew up the skywalk by using blood magic," I said. "Roxanne placed your body in stasis, but whatever you did is serious. She said we need serious firepower to deal with the damage you did to yourself."

"I need to go deal with Evers," Monty said. "I'm sure Roxanne is overreacting; it's the doctor side of her. I'm fine."

"Doubt it," I said. "Take a moment and assess, why don't you?"

"I don't need to 'assess'," Monty answered, raising his voice. "I'm fine."

"We are going to Kali," I said. "I'm not a mage, and even I can sense your energy is all over the place, probably worse than mine."

"Rubbish. You're probably picking up on the ambient energy of this place."

"Humor me," I said. "If you try to cast a teleportation

circle, I'll tell my cute hellhound puppy to latch onto your leg and keep you in place."

"This is a Zegna," he said, pointing to his suit. "You wouldn't dare."

"It's not like you haven't ruined suits in the past," I said, staring at Monty. "What's a little hellhound slobber on a bespoke suit? It has healing properties. It's good for you, like sunshine."

"I hadn't realized you had become a mage doctor during my incapacitation."

"Didn't need to," I said. "I had access to a sorceress doctor...assess please."

"Fine. If you insist on this ludicrous theory of my being a hair's breadth away from a schism, I will oblige your insanity."

"Please do," I said, waving him on. "Try not to take all day. I have a goddess of destruction to convince."

Monty sat down on the marble floor and crossed his legs. He closed his eyes and slowed his breathing.

"This will take but a moment."

"Remember, no casting," I said. "I'm serious."

"As am I," he replied. "I will show you I'm perfectly fine."

"Nothing more I would prefer to hear than you being fine."

He became silent for a few seconds, focusing on his breathing. After a moment, he opened his eyes. It didn't look good, but I wanted to hear him say it.

"As I said, this diagnosis is just another example of Roxanne's overprotective...bollocks."

"Roxanne has overprotective bollocks?" I asked. "Is there something I should know?"

"She's right," Monty said, his voice tight with tension. "If I cast, it could set off a chain reaction causing a schism. How did I miss that?"

"This schism thing is where you go dark and become Monty the Terrible?" I asked. "I mean that's what Roxanne said would happen."

"A schism would increase my power considerably and cause me to go dark...yes."

"Turning you into a Sith mage?"

"There's no such thing as a Sith mage," Monty said. "It would, however, affect my thought processes, with an inclination towards more uninhibited acts."

"Uninhibited...do you mean, evil?"

"I mean, with a lack of any moral compass. I would take an action because it suited or benefitted me, without consideration for how my actions may impact others."

"Would you be dangerous?"

"Imagine my uncle without a moral compass."

"Um...he's dating the Morrigan," I answered. "I'd say his compass is a bit off already."

"True, his taste in partners is questionable at best, but his moral compass, his sense of right and wrong, is unwavering," Monty answered. "If he lost that and went dark...I doubt all of the Ten could stop him, and you've seen some of them in action."

"You would become that strong?"

"Stronger. Darkness is easy to underestimate and will overcome you without you even knowing it," Monty said. "It is enticing, captivating, and alluring. Even the strongest mage must fight that internal battle...daily."

"You just described becoming a Sith. Are you sure there aren't any Sith mages out there?"

"Certain," Monty said. "This isn't some science fiction fantasy. When a mage goes dark, it's very unlikely they return to the light. Usually, the Black Orchid must step in and terminate."

"I heard. So, Roxanne was right?" I asked, making sure. "You cast and you're toast?"

"Whoever rigged the skywalk—Evers—placed runes that would accelerate a schism if I tried to cast," Monty replied, while standing up. "I cast, and a schism is likely."

"Can you undo the damage?" I asked. "Prevent the schism from happening?"

"No," Monty said. "It would be like asking a surgeon to operate on himself. He could start an incision, but it would go pear-shaped from there."

"Roxanne said we need serious firepower to fix whatever it is."

"She's correct," Monty said with a nod, as he sat on the bench. "Evers outmaneuvered me in every step of this. All I can tell is that she used lost runes to set this trap. We'd need power beyond an Archmage. We'd need a..."

"A god...or goddess in this case."

TWENTY-SEVEN

"Kali is a particularly dangerous goddess," Monty said, walking next to me as we approached the doorway. "It may be best to let me do the talking."

"I'm skilled in non-destructive diplomacy, unlike some mages I know."

"I've seen no evidence of your diplomatic expertise," Monty answered. "This isn't a joke, Simon. If things go sideways, and they usually do, I can't cast or do much to help, outside of using my swords."

"It's not going to come to that, trust me. Besides, no one wants to hear your creepy, wailing swords."

"How do you know this portal will work?"

"Karma said it would, why would she lie?"

"But how? It's not like you can cast. Is it tied to you somehow? To your mark?"

"I think it's because I'm the Chosen of Kali." I said. "I didn't get into the 'how' so much, just the what. If she says it'll work, I think it will."

"You would make a terrible mage," Monty said, as we

stood in front of the last archway. "Mages—*I*—don't operate on blind faith. We need to know the inner workings of things. We always ask for the how first."

The mark on my hand began giving off golden light again. In the archway, suspended in mid-air hung a large, golden endless knot made of faintly glowing light.

"I'm thinking that's the door we need, and my mark is the how," I said. "You ready?"

"Hardly, but I don't see an alternative," Monty said. "This may be our only opportunity to rectify both of our situations."

"My thoughts exactly," I said, placing my glowing hand in the large endless knot hanging in front of us. "I hope this works."

The glow from my hand expanded and traveled to the suspended design. The light from my hand raced along the larger endless knot as it expanded and filled the archway. Within seconds it was gone. In its absence stood a large, stone door, covered in runes. In the center of the door was another endless knot, pulsing faintly with orange light.

I grabbed the handle and Monty grabbed my arm.

"It could be rigged to detonate," he said. "Slowly."

"If I open it slowly, does that mean the explosion will happen slowly too?" I asked, opening the door normally. "See? No explosion. Not everyone walks around with a blast radius, like a certain mage I know. Let's go."

We stepped through the door, and found ourselves in a large courtyard.

"I'm getting a serious Inception feel here," I said, looking around. "This is the temple, inside of a temple, inside of a building. It's like a crazy nesting doll of temples."

Monty remained silent and slowly turned, looking around the courtyard.

"This is the Kailasa temple, but I don't recall many of these engravings," Monty said, examining one of the nearby walls. "This location feels much older than Kailasa."

We stood in the U-shaped courtyard of a stone temple complex cut out of the side of a mountain stone. On three sides, the mountainside towered above us. In the center of the cutout sat the temple. Like the mandir in Jersey, every inch of the stone temple was covered in intricate designs.

Stone obelisks and columns were cut into the surrounding mountain. There were images of elephants, lions, and turtles, along with depictions of dancing goddesses all around the temple.

The dark stone looked weathered with age, but all of the designs were clear and easily seen. None of them were missing parts, nothing was chipped or broken. I could sense energy emanating from the temple. What really threw me was the size and scope of the work. This temple was easily three times the size of the mandir in Jersey, and every bit as ornate and intricate.

"How did they get the stone up the mountain?" I said, looking out at the opening of the courtyard. "That must have been some amount of carrying."

"They didn't need to carry any of the stone," Monty said. "It was all here."

"They quarried the stone from the mountain?"

"No, the temple is one solid piece carved out from the mountain. The artisans carved what they wanted, working top down, and excavated the excess."

"How did they manage that?" I asked, amazed. "I can't even imagine that now with our technology."

"I'm sure Shiva probably had something to do with it," Monty said, pointing ahead. "Those statues to the left of the entrance are Shaivaite—based on Shiva. The ones on the right are Vaishnavaites—based on Vishnu."

"What, no Kali? In her own temple?"

"Kali and Shiva are intimately linked," Monty said. "I wouldn't be surprised if images of her aren't spread out over the complex. This is, however, a Shiva temple, judging from the central shrine. Are you certain we're in the right place?"

"You're asking like I was driving the Dark Goat here," I said. "If we're here, this is the right place."

A roar filled the temple complex. Monty drew his crying swords and I unholstered Grim Whisper.

"What are you doing?" I asked. "Those crying swords are only going to attract attention."

"They're not crying swords, they're Sorrows, and that roar was probably the temple guard."

"The temple guard feel the urge to roar when they're patrolling the grounds?"

"They do when they're Rakshasas," Monty said. "You do remember them? Kali's bodyguards and first line of defense?"

"How I am supposed to forget them?" I hissed. "Those things were hideous."

"Don't forget lethal," Monty added. "One would think the 'Chosen of Kali' would get some kind of preferential treatment in her temple."

"Oh, ha ha, good to see that stasis hasn't frozen your brain in place," I said, looking around the corner. "I don't think Kali is the welcoming type. You don't get to be called the Destroyer by being warm and cuddly."

"Good point," Monty said. "Well, we're here. Where to?"

"How should I know?" I said with a shrug. "How about we find the place with the scariest vibe?"

"Find the place with the scariest vibe?" Monty mocked. "That's your plan?"

"Hey, I got us here while you were taking a stasis nap," I shot back. "I'm the one that had to dodge an orb of death while you were busy playing rescue with Roxanne."

"Playing rescue?" he answered, raising his voice. "Playing rescue?"

"Did I stutter?" I asked, as one of the Rakshasas rounded the corner. "Oh shit, were we too loud?"

"You were," Monty said. "I was merely asking what the next step was when you lost control, thus attracting the attention of this monstrosity of mayhem."

I glared at Monty, but had to dodge to the side to avoid the lumbering beast swiping a set of razor sharp claws in my direction.

"These things are still as ugly as I remember," I said, taking aim. "I still prefer the tiger versions. Am I imagining things, or is this one bigger than the ones we fought before?"

Rakshasas were a mash-up of every child's worst nightmare. They came equipped with huge fangs that would make a saber-tooth proud, and claws that would give even Wolverine a run for his money. As it stared at me, its eyes pulsed neon red, like the moment right before one of Peaches' baleful glares.

Around its neck it wore a polished silver chain. From

the chain hung a glowing violet orb about the size of a grapefruit. Runes covered its body and these too glowed with a faint violet light.

"These appear to be stronger than the ones we encountered," Monty said, holding the swords in a guard stance. "It's certainly larger."

"Oh," I said, sliding across the courtyard with Peaches in tow. "What gave it away?"

"The orb around its neck is exponentially more potent than the ones we faced," Monty answered. "I also don't recall them being covered in runes."

"Rhetorical question!" I yelled as I rolled to one side to avoid a foot stomp, and then had to dodge backwards, causing the creature to narrowly miss making me half the man I was. "Need a little help here."

Monty clashed his swords together, causing the Rakshasa to momentarily turn in his direction with a growl, before returning its focus on me.

"Why is it staring at me?" I asked, firing twice before ducking behind a stone obelisk to avoid another swipe. It sheared off a section of the obelisk as if it had been made of paper. "Not a fan of the attention. FYI watch the claws...they're sharp."

"Perhaps they only zero in on the 'Chosen of Kali'?" Monty said from behind another obelisk. "Maybe they're your welcoming committee."

"Not...feeling...welcome," I said, moving around another column and down a passageway...into the line of sight of another Rakshasa. It sniffed the air around it, then locked onto me. "Really not feeling welcome."

I pressed the main bead on my mala bracelet, activating my shield.

"Entropy rounds seem ineffective," Monty yelled out. "You may need your blade."

"Pass," I said. "No way am I getting that close to those claws."

<Can I bite them?>

<Shred but don't chew. These monsters are nasty. Don't let them hit you with those claws either.>

<I'm hungry, but I'm not that hungry.>

<Good boy. Stay close to Monty. He can't use his powers.>

<Did he break his magic?>

I almost chuckled at the remark. If it hadn't been for the massive fist bearing down on my location, I would have. I barely had time to react, and raised my arm with the shield. The force of the impact launched me across the courtyard. I had two thoughts as I sailed across the temple complex: How did something so large move so fast that it snuck up on me, and this was going to hurt.

I smashed into the mountain on the other side of the courtyard, dropping to the ground a second later with the wind knocked out of me.

"Ow," I said with a groan. "Last time I fly Rakshasa airlines."

"The orbs, Simon," Monty called out, as I heard his sword parry and deflect claws. "Destroy the orbs."

"Got it," I said. "I hear your sob story swords. I'm heading to you."

I circled around the closest monster, and dashed between two obelisks as I made my way to Monty. I peeked around the corner to see him deflect, slide to the side and slash with one of his swords. They may as well have been made of cardboard for all the damage they did.

"Feel free to jump in any time," Monty said, ducking

under a swipe and stepping behind a wall that became rubble, a few Rakshasa punches later. "It's not like I'm in danger of evisceration or anything."

"Well, when you put it that way," I said, running towards the creature closest to Monty. "Distract it."

I rolled to the side as Monty stepped in, plunging a Sorrow into its flank. The creature roared in pain, swinging an arm and nearly decapitating Monty. I materialized Ebonsoul, took a breath, and plunged the blade into the violet orb around the Rakshasa's neck.

The orb shattered into dust as Ebonsoul continued downward into the creature's massive chest. Violet energy exploded outward from its runes and siphoned into Ebonsoul.

The creature roared one last time before falling to its knees and then collapsing, reverted to dust a few seconds later. In my hand, Ebonsoul vibrated with violet energy. The runes along its length glowed red and violet as I looked up to see real fear in Monty's eyes.

"Simon, let go of the blade," Monty hissed, reabsorbing his own blades. "You have to let it go, that's too much energy for your unstable signature!"

"What do you think I'm trying to do?" I yelled back. "I can't let go!"

Another Rakshasa rounded the corner, bearing down on me, and I felt time dilate. Monty had made the decision before I could react.

"No," he whispered softly, and outstretched an arm. "You will not touch him."

A beam of black and red energy shot from Monty's hand and blasted the creature in the chest, obliterating it. Another Rakshasa appeared, and Monty unleashed a barrage of orbs that punched into its body, disintegrating it where it stood. Two more monsters dropped down from one of the shrines on either side of us, claws drawn.

Monty extended both arms in their direction.

"Monty, no!" I yelled, "Don't!"

It was too late.

Two more beams of black energy shot from his hands, the red was nowhere to be seen. They slammed into the remaining Rakshasas, blasting them into the far wall of the courtyard. Even after they had been launched, Monty kept blasting them until there were only two large craters where the creatures had been seconds before.

Monty fell to his knees grabbing his head. It was the schism.

"You need...you need to stay away, Simon."

"We're here," I pleaded. "We can find Kali and she can help you. Just hold on!"

"I...can't...my skull feels like it's splitting," Monty said, through gritted teeth. He looked up at me, and I could see the despair in his eyes. "It's too late."

"Kali! Where are you?" I screamed, turning to the walls of the courtyard. "Show yourself!"

"Don't...don't come...after me," Monty said, as I felt the surge of energy build up behind me. "Stay away from me, Simon. I...don't know...what I could do."

I turned to see Monty in the center of a black teleportation circle. The runes along its edges raced around its circumference.

"Monty, no," I said, keeping my voice calm. "It's me. Hold on."

The sclera of his eyes had become shot through with

black veins. Black energy raced along his body and funneled into the teleportation circle.

"If you seek me out," Monty said, his voice strange, "I will end your immortal existence."

I ran to the circle as it exploded in black energy.

TWENTY-EIGHT

"Monty!" I came to my senses with a start, hoping it was all a nightmare. "Monty!"

Peaches sat by my side and gave off a low whine.

"He is gone," said a female voice behind me. "Are you certain you want to pursue him? He has become consumed by darkness."

I recognized the voice.

Kali.

"Where were you?" I said, whirling in her direction. "You could have saved him!"

"You are in my domain," she said, her eyes glowing a deep violet. "You will show respect."

"You want to know what I think about your *respect?*" I said, standing as I seethed in my fury at losing my friend and family. "You and your *respect* can go fu..."

She waved a hand, and I became an instant ballistic missile, hurtling towards the mountain at speed. I smashed backfirst into the wall, shattering every bone in my back.

My body became an inferno as it tried to mitigate the damage with ample doses of agony.

I remained adhered to the wall, twenty feet off the ground, as Kali walked over to where I was and looked up. She then floated gently into the air until we were eye to eye.

"You were saying?" she asked.

I could barely see through the pain, but the rage coursing through my body was stronger.

"You...let him...you let him become dark," I managed. "You could've saved him."

"I let him?" Kali said. "He did not ask for permission."

"What are you saying? Are you saying he wanted to go dark?"

"I'm saying, he made his choice, Simon."

"He was saving me from one of your monsters."

"Which you managed to kill," Kali added. "You didn't appear to need saving. You wielded enough power to end the threat on your own. You still do."

Kali didn't appear like the many-armed goddess I was so used to seeing in images of her. She was dressed in a loose-fitting, magenta robe, finished with golden brocade. Indecipherable orange runes flowed around its surface. Her black hair danced around her head, pushed by an invisible wind, and her blue skin glistened with a deep undercurrent of power.

I was held immobile against the wall where she had smashed me. The presence of an enormous weight pressed against my body prohibited any major movement. The amount of energy I sensed from her was indescribable. I realized in that moment, that she could have erased me from existence with a thought.

"You could've helped him," I said with a struggle. It felt like two or three elephants were sitting on me. "Why didn't you help him?"

"He didn't want help...he wanted power."

"No," I said. "Monty is not after power. He is better than that."

"Is he?" Kali asked. "He knew what would happen if he chose to cast. You yourself warned him several times."

"He was saving me."

"No," Kali said. "Open your eye"—she pointed to her forehead—"he made a choice."

"No, it was Evers—she put something in the runes at the skywalk," I said. "Something that influenced him, made him go dark."

"It's not that simple. He wasn't forced to cast or to go dark. He made a choice."

"To save me."

"To save you?" she answered with a laugh. "You weren't the one that needed saving."

"What are you saying?" I asked, confused. "What do you mean?"

"Why are you here, 'Chosen of Kali'? A horrible title by the way," she said. "I much prefer 'Kali's Cursed'."

"I didn't pick it," I said, trying to shift my arm to scratch my nose. "Do you think we could have this conversation somewhere non-crater like?"

"If you can understand what respect means, possibly."

"I apologize," I said. "I was angry, frustrated and confused. Still am. I meant no disrespect."

"It seems you *can* learn," Kali said with a nod, as we slowly descended to the ground. "It took some head pounding, but something made it into that thick skull of yours."

"What did you mean by 'You, weren't the one that needed saving'?"

"Will you go after your friend?" Kali asked, forming benches out of the stone as we landed. They formed under us, and we sat opposite each other with a small table between us. I had to make sure they were stone because the bench felt soft, like a large cushion. "He has made it clear he will attempt to kill you if you do so."

"Yes," I said without hesitation. "He is my friend and my family. I'm still going after him and bringing him back to his senses."

"Very well," she said with a nod. "You have one question...ask."

"One question?"

Kali raised an eyebrow.

"Wait, wait, that wasn't the question," I said, quickly holding up a hand. "I can ask anything? Again, not the question, just trying to determine the parameters here."

"One question, and I will answer. Choose wisely."

"How do I bring Monty back from being dark?"

"A good question," she said. "Worthy of a friend and shieldbearer. I will answer this question and then send you on your way. Return to my domain at your peril."

"Can we do it without a teleportation circle? They don't agree with me."

"The answer you are seeking is contained within the ripples of purpose," she said, making no sense. "Open your purpose, and you can help your friend find his way back to the light."

"That doesn't really make sense," I said after a pause. "Can I get a do-over?"

"Would you like me to smash you into the wall again?"

"No, thanks," I said. "I'll figure it out."

"I truly hope you do," she said, her eyes gleaming with power. "Goodbye, Simon, Kali's Cursed."

She nodded slightly, and the temple disappeared in a violet flash.

<Can you bring me some meat?>

Peaches had dropped his bowl at my feet. He missed my toes by an inch. It took me a second to get my bearings. I was back in our office and Monty was still missing. Shit.

<Is meat all you think about?>

<Is there anything else? Meat is the most important thing. Meat is Life.>

<Monty is missing, boy. That's more important than meat.>

<Nothing is more important than meat.>

<This is. Monty is family. The same way we are bondmates. Monty is part of the pack. Part of my pack.>

<Then we will find him. Right after I eat my meat. Ask the lady in the big room if she is going to help.>

<The who in the what?>

<Did the powerful lady break your head against the wall?>

<My head is fine. Are you saying someone is in the conference room?>

<Yes, she smells nice and powerful.>

I drew Grim Whisper and made my way to the conference room. Sitting in the chair farthest from the door, was a woman.

She was dressed in a black leather jacket that was a cross

between police uniform and combat armor. Her short, black hair framed her pale face. Green eyes stared at me over the mug—*my* mug—of coffee she was drinking. Next to her on the table, sat the hourglass Evers had materialized, the sand slowly descending. The runically charged sand had turned black. Red energy pulsing around the hourglass.

On the woman's lap was the largest black cat I'd ever seen. If she pulled a Bond villain and started petting it while issuing threats, I would feel obligated to shoot first, then ask questions.

She put my mug down, and slowly reached into her jacket, pulling out a small card.

"Who are you?" I asked, aiming at her with Grim Whisper—which didn't seem to faze her at all. "Why are you in my home?"

She picked up my mug, took another sip of coffee and slowly pushed the card forward.

"My name is Jessikah Onuris, Black Orchid, Farsight Division."

"This is relevant to me because...?" I asked, picking up her card and confirming the information she had just shared. The card was a made of thin metal, with the etching of her name and position over the silhouette of a feline head on one side, and on the other, a flower I could only assume was an orchid. "Anyone can have one of these made." I tossed the card back on the table. "Are you serious?"

"Not like that one," Jessikah said, retrieving the card and putting it back into her jacket pocket. "Those are only given to officers of the Orchid."

"Why are you here?"

"I'm here to apprehend one Tristan Montague, dark mage and practitioner of blood magic."

"Apprehend or terminate?"

"That depends on him," she said. "Do you know of his whereabouts?"

"Even if I did, and I don't, what makes you think I would tell you?"

"Because I know you want to save him," she said. "Because he's a victim here. You see this hourglass? It's a darkglass. I've seen it used before. The last mage to fall into her trap wasn't so lucky...we found him too late. Tristan still has time."

"What happens if the sand runs out?" I said, dreading the answer. "How long does he have?"

"Three to four days max," Jessikah said. "If the sand runs out before we find him, my orders change from apprehension to termination."

"I won't let you kill him."

"Then I suggest you help me find him so it doesn't come to that."

"How do I know you want to help him? I heard Black Orchid was the mage police. You guys are a glorified hit squad."

"The only people who say that are those who don't know our true purpose," she said. "Especially that of the Farsight Division. I can't force you to help me, but if you do, I can find him with enough time left to reverse his condition. If not, I may catch up to him when he's run out of time and options. Either way, with or without your assistance, I will find him. It's your choice if I stop him or drop him."

"You will not be dropping him."

"Then help me find him while we can still stop him. Before it's too late."

"He's much stronger now," I said, processing her words. "How do I know you have the firepower?"

"I'm very capable at what I do, Mr. Strong. Help me do my job and we can save him. Stand in my way, and you jeopardize his life, as well as your own."

"My life is rarely in jeopardy, trust me."

"Get in my way and it will be."

"You let me speak to him first. You take no aggressive action against him until I've had a chance to speak to him," I said. "You want my help? Those are my conditions. You can accept them, or you can see yourself out."

She took another sip of coffee, looked down at her beast of a cat and nodded.

"Those conditions are acceptable," she said. "How soon can you mobilize?"

"I'm already headed out the door," I shot back, leaving the conference room. "Keep up."

THE END

AUTHOR NOTES

Thank you for reading this story and jumping back into the Monty & Strong World.

It wasn't intentional.

No, really. It wasn't. Even with an outline (which I had) and a clear trajectory (which I could see), the story pulled a left when I wanted to go right. I knew Monty had to 'dark' from the onset of this book (and series). It's been simmering for a few stories now. His use of blood magic, various circumstances providing an opening for its use, and even way back, when he cast a void vortex (not one, but two) in the city. We knew this was coming at some point. Does it make it easier? No, no it doesn't.

It was bound to happen, but it needed to happen the way it happened in this book. It needed to happen first by Monty saving Roxanne, by protecting Simon, and then by facing his past in Evers. I'd like to say I saw it coming in this book, except I didn't. Yes, I had the idea, but around chapter 20 I could see where things were going, and I pulled an authorial VETO on the whole idea.

It went pretty much like this:

"Not like this," I said. "It has to happen another way. Plus, it's going to leave too much story untold. This is going to cause some waves...tsunami type waves."

"I know," the story said. "Means you better get started on the next story NOW."

"This is NOT the ending I had in mind...this isn't even an ending!"

"All endings are just beginnings, this is the ending for this PART of the story. Now get writing. This is getting weird."

That is how DARK GLASS ended up where it did. I did try to wrangle it back to where I wanted it to go (several times), but it was unruly and didn't flow. This meant I needed to go where the story dictated I go. It wasn't pleasant, or easy, but it was necessary.

This circumstance doesn't happen often (Michiko's stories were intentional cliffs) especially not with Monty & Simon. The last time I had an ending like this, was back in BLOOD IS THICKER. The original version of that ending nearly caused me bodily harm. This ending, while not as severe, is one of those endings that make you want to lob curses (and kindles) in my direction. I understand, I truly do, but it needed to happen. My apologies.

All of that being said, it's getting exciting. Monty's past is coming back to look for some vengeance. If you read WAR MAGE, you will have some background on what happened during the war. The next book goes in depth as Monty wrestles with what it means to be 'dark'. We also get to meet a member of the new Black Orchid—Jessikah Onuris. She will be a pivotal figure in this story before spinning off into her own series later on.

Simon will have to make some hard choices. There are

forces out there that would prefer a dark Monty and a dead Simon. These forces are actively working towards that outcome. The choices Simon makes will have repercussions going forward. You will see him evolve in his ability, and increase in fear, as he realizes the world he inhabits is becoming even more lethal.

The events of DARK GLASS are happening simultaneously with the events of Rule of the Council-Michiko's story. Shortly after this book goes live, BLOOD RULE the third part of Rule of the Council, will be completed adding an interesting dimension to the next M&S book-WALKING THE RAZOR.

In each story I have the privilege of writing, I try to reveal more about the character backgrounds and lives. Sometimes this creates more questions than answers. I promise I will get to all of the questions...eventually.

Things are going to ramp up fairly fast in the next few M&S books with the pace being fast & furious. Strap in. If we were on a rollercoaster, DARK GLASS is us reaching the top of the first crest. The slow climb, the anticipation, and the dread of the drop are all there.

Hold on tight, the drop is just ahead. I feel the butterflies in the pit of my stomach. It's going to be amazing, scary, and exciting all at once. I hope you continue joining me on this wild ride.

Thank you again for taking the time to read this story and your incredible patience. I wrote it for you and I hope you enjoyed spending some time getting in trouble with Trio of Terror.

If you enjoyed this story—please leave a review. It's really important and helps the book (and me).

If you've read this far (and I hope you have), I've

included the first chapter of the next M&S book-WALKING THE RAZOR.

Read on to see what happens next.

Thank you again for jumping into this adventure with me.

WALKING THE RAZOR-ONE

I stepped out of the conference room and into a green flash.

Grim Whisper was in my hand a split second later.

"Put that thing away, boy, before you hurt someone. Starting with you."

It was Dex. An angry sounding Dex.

I holstered my weapon and realized Dex wasn't alone, which would've been bad enough. Two figures stood next to him. I squinted as my eyes adjusted to the aftereffects of the teleportation circle Dex used.

TK and LD stood next to Dex. LD gave me a quick look of sympathy that said 'brace yourself', while TK glared at me as if I had broken into Fordey and stolen an artifact of value. It wasn't a good look. On the glare-o-meter, not even a Clint Glint could withstand TK's withering gaze.

"You didn't think to call us?" TK said, her voice slicing through the air like a scalpel through skin. "You actually thought it best to tackle this on your own?"

I looked at LD who shook his head.

"Monty said not to call you?" I answered knowing it was the wrong answer. "It was his idea. He said it would protect you."

"Protect us?" TK replied and I took a step back. Her two words expressed anger, disappointment, and more anger. She was pissed. "He can barely protect himself."

"Are you daft, boy? Dex said, placing a gentle hand on my shoulder. "We should have been the first on the scene. Now you have to deal with"—Dex glanced at Jessikah —"the Black Orchid."

He said the sect name like a curse.

"Whoa," I said, raising my hands. "I didn't call her either. She just showed up."

"They usually do," TK said. "Like mold or an unwanted growth."

Dex stepped around me and looked at Jessikah closely.

"Farsight Division?" he asked, pointing at the large black cat. "Daughter of Bast. Well, at least they're taking this seriously."

Jessikah stood frozen in place, her expression one of shock. The cool, collected, Black Orchid agent had left the building. In her place, stood an awestruck mage rookie. To her credit, she regained her composure almost immediately.

"Yes sir," Jessikah said. For second I thought she was going to salute. "Farsight Division and a Daughter of Bast."

"Good for you," Dex answered. "You can leave now. This is a family matter, and you are *not* family. We'll take it from here."

"I'm afraid I can't do that, sir," Jessikah answered, demonstrating how much she enjoyed living dangerously. "My superiors..."

"Can go suck an egg," Dex finished. "Who was it? Which Elder from the Orchid sent you?"

"All of them, sir."

"Ach, they must still be upset," Dex said, shaking his head. "Mages with their fragile egos and petty grudges. The war is a distant memory."

"Not to them," Jessikah answered. "They still remember."

"Of course they do," TK said. "It's difficult to forget, much less forgive, a humiliation."

"No matter," Dex answered gruffly, with a wave of his hand. "Your services are no longer required. Miss...?"

"Jessikah, sir. Jessikah Onuris."

"Onuris?" TK said, with a slight look of surprise. "You're Gregor's child?"

"He's my father, yes," Jessikah said. "You are TK and LD from Fordey Boutique. The Orchid speaks highly of you."

"Only those that don't know us," LD said with a smile. "I'm sure your Elders say otherwise."

"They do," Jessikah said, looking away. "They call you dangerous rogue mages. A threat to every sect, and...worse things."

LD smiled and nodded.

"That sounds about right," LD said. "They're breathing today to insult us because of how dangerous we are, and the things we did...for them."

"Gregor was a formidable mage," TK said, examining

Jessikah. "Not overly skilled, but a diligent student. He excelled by outworking his peers."

"You...you taught my father?"

"Of course not," TK replied with a slight smile. "I taught the person who taught your father."

"Doesn't matter who she is," Dex said with a growl. "Her services are no longer needed. Go back and tell them Dexter Montague said so."

Jessikah reached into her pocket and pulled out a black envelope. She handed it to a wary Dex, who took it with one eyebrow raised.

"They told me to give this to you when you 'made your appearance' to stop me."

Dex grumbled something under his breath and opened the envelope. Standing beside him, I managed to get a look at the letter. The paper was a light grey color and the flowing script was in blood red ink. The top of the letter was adorned by the same image of a black orchid that I noticed on the rear Jessikah's card. They took their branding seriously it seemed.

To the esteemed Dexter Montague,

If you are reading this letter, you have no doubt attempted to dissuade our mage from performing her duties as an agent of the Black Orchid.

This is a formal missive to notify you that we are operating within our jurisdiction. Your nephew, Tristan Montague, has been under observation for some time now. The casting of void vortices inside a populated city, not to mention the devastation he and his partner visited upon London has not gone unnoticed.

The Penumbra Consortium is actively using back channels to have him erased, declaring him to be a menace to humanity and all historical structures of import. Understanding your propensity for the disregard of rules, regulations, or any semblance of order, we are certain the Penumbra Consortium and their petition cause you little to no concern.

With this understanding we are prepared to take the following steps and inform you:

If our agent, Jessikah Onuris of the Farsight Division is hindered in her investigation of one Tristan Montague by you or any of the rogue mages that comprise the group known as 'The Ten' we will consider it a violation of sect law.

To that end, we will enforce dissolution of the Golden Circle sect, as is our right, if we feel this violation has occurred. To convey this is plain speech, keep your nose out of this one or it will be broken and bloodied. We will do what must be done, and if you interfere in any way, shape, or form, we will remove the Golden Circle from existence with extreme prejudice and overwhelming force.

With the utmost sincerity and resolve,

The Black Orchid Elders

I saw Dex get angrier by the second as he read the letter again, before handing it to TK.

"Those bloody shits!" Dex yelled as Peaches whined and moved closer to my leg. He stared at the now startled and scared Jessikah. "They dare to threaten me? My nephew? The Golden Circle?"

To be fair, Dex was scary even when he was happy. He always had an undercurrent of danger and insanity mixed into a package of magexuberance. In his current state, he stepped way beyond scary, and planted both feet firmly in petrifyingly frightening territory. I could see why the Morrigan would be attracted. The power coming off of him was palpable as his energy signature rose.

"This will be a problem," TK said looking at LD. "It

would be a good idea if Dex got some air while we explore the details."

LD escorted Dex outside.

TK turned and focused all of her attention on Jessikah.

SPECIAL MENTIONS

Larry & Tammy—The WOUF: because even when you aren't there...you're there.

Larry : because Simon has PTSD - Post Traumatic Stress of Dentistry.

Orlandtastic: because Sunny is determined and stubborn and said so. That's why.

Jim Ball: because of Barkour, Peaches' favorite pastime.

Diane Kassmann: for introducing me to the concept of paraprosdokians, specifically this one: "I don't want to hurt you, but it's still on my list."

Dawn McQueen Mortimer: Psst it's spelled MacLeod. Thank you, lol!

Jo Dungey: for the Duesenberg Coupé Simone Midnight Ghost. Do I need to say anything else? No, I do not.

Orlando A. Sanchez
www.orlandoasanchez.com

Orlando has been writing ever since his teens when he was immersed in creating scenarios for playing Dungeons and Dragons with his friends every weekend.

The worlds of his books are urban settings with a twist of the paranormal lurking just behind the scenes and with generous doses of magic, martial arts, and mayhem.

He currently resides in Queens, NY with his wife and children.

BITTEN PEACHES PUBLISHING

Thanks for Reading

If you enjoyed this book, would you please **leave a review** at the site you purchased it from? It doesn't have to be long... just a line or two would be fantastic and it would really help me out.

Bitten Peaches Publishing offers more books by this author. From science fiction & fantasy to adventure & mystery, we bring the best stories for adults and kids alike.

www.BittenPeachesPublishing.com

More books by Orlando A. Sanchez

The Warriors of the Way

The Karashihan*•The Spiritual Warriors•The Ascendants•The Fallen Warrior•The Warrior Ascendant•The Master Warrior

John Kane

The Deepest Cut*•Blur

Sepia Blue

The Last Dance*•Rise of the Night•Sisters•Nightmare

Chronicles of the Modern Mystics

The Dark Flame•A Dream of Ashes

Montague & Strong Detective Agency Novels

Tombyards & Butterflies•Full Moon Howl•Blood is Thicker•Silver Clouds Dirty Sky•Homecoming•Dragons & Demigods•Bullets & Blades•Hell Hath No Fury•Reaping Wind•The Golem•Dark Glass

Montague & Strong Detective Agency Stories

No God is Safe•The Date•The War Mage•A Proper Hellhound•The Perfect Cup•Saving Mr. K

Brew & Chew Adventures

Hellhound Blues

Night Warden Novels

Wander•ShadowStrut

Division 13

The Operative•The Magekiller

Blackjack Chronicles

The Dread Warlock

The Assassin's Apprentice

The Birth of Death

Gideon Shepherd Thrillers

Sheepdog

DAMNED

Aftermath

RULE OF THE COUNCIL

Blood Ascension•Blood Betrayal•Blood Rule

*Books denoted with an asterisk are **FREE** via my website—www.orlandoasanchez.com

ACKNOWLEDEGEMENTS

With each book, I realize that every time I learn something about this craft, it highlights so many things I still have to learn. Each book, each creative expression, has a large group of people behind it.

This book is no different.

Even though you see one name on the cover, it is with the knowledge that I am standing on the shoulders of the literary giants that informed my youth, and am supported by my generous readers who give of their time to jump into the adventures of my overactive imagination.

I would like to take a moment to express my most sincere thanks:

To Dolly: my wife and greatest support. You make all this possible each and every day. You keep me grounded when I get lost in the forest of ideas. Thank you for asking the right questions when needed, and listening intently when I go off on tangents. Thank you for who you are and the space you create—I love you.

To my Tribe: You are the reason I have stories to tell. You cannot possibly fathom how much and how deeply I love you all.

To Lee: Because you were the first audience I ever had. I love you, sis.

To the Logsdon Family: The words, *thank you* are insufficient to describe the gratitude in my heart for each of you. JL your support always demands I bring my best, my A-game, and produce the best story I can. Both you and Lorelei (my Uber Jeditor) and now, Audrey, are the reason I am where I am today. My thank you for the notes, challenges, corrections, advice, and laughter. Your patience is truly infinite. *Arigatogozaimasu.*

To The Montague & Strong Case Files Group-AKA The MoB (Mages of Badassery): When I wrote T&B there were fifty-five members in The MoB. As of this release, there are over one thousand three hundred members in the MoB. I am honored to be able to call you my MoB Family. Thank you for being part of this group and M&S.

You make this possible. **THANK YOU.**

To the ever-vigilant PACK: You help make the MoB... the MoB. Keeping it a safe place for us to share and just...

be. Thank you for your selfless vigilance. You truly are the Sentries of Sanity.

Chris Christman II: A real life technomancer who makes the **MoBTV LIVEvents +Kaffeeklatsch** on YouTube amazing. Thank you for your tireless work and wisdom. Everything is connected...you totally rock!

To the WTA-The Incorrigibles: JL, Ben Z. Eric QK., S.S., and Noah.

They sound like a bunch of badass misfits, because they are. My exposure to the deranged and deviant brain trust you all represent helped me be the author I am today. I have officially gone to the *dark side* thanks to all of you. I humbly give you my thanks, and...it's all your fault.

To my fellow Indie Authors, specifically the tribe at 20books to 50k: Thank you for creating a space where authors can feel listened to, and encouraged to continue on this path. A rising tide lifts all the ships indeed.

To The English Advisory: Aaron, Penny, Carrie, Davina, and all of the UK MoB. For all things English...thank you.

To DEATH WISH COFFEE: This book (and every book I write) has been fueled by generous amounts of the only coffee on the planet (and in space) strong enough to power my very twisted imagination. Is there any other coffee that can compare? I think not. DEATHWISH-thank you!

To Deranged Doctor Design: Kim, Darja, Tanja, Jovana, and Milo (Designer Extraordinaire).

If you've seen the covers of my books and been amazed, you can thank the very talented and gifted creative team at DDD. They take the rough ideas I give them, and produce incredible covers that continue to surprise and amaze me. Each time, I find myself striving to write a story worthy of the covers they produce. DDD you embody professionalism and creativity. Thank you for the great service and spectacular covers. **YOU GUYS RULE!**

To you, the reader: I was always taught to save the best for last. I write these stories for **you**. Thank you for jumping down the rabbit holes of ***what if?*** with me. You are the reason I write the stories I do.

You keep reading...I'll keep writing.

Thank you for your support and encouragement.

CONTACT ME

I really do appreciate your feedback. You can let me know what you thought of the story by emailing me at:
orlando@orlandoasanchez.com

To get **FREE** stories please visit my page at:
www.orlandoasanchez.com

For more information on the M&S World...come join the MoB Family on Facebook!
You can find us at:
Montague & Strong Case Files

Visit our online M&S World Swag Store located at:
Emandes

If you enjoyed the book, **please leave a review**. Reviews help the book, and also help other readers find good stories to read.

THANK YOU!

ART SHREDDERS

No book is the work of one person. I am fortunate enough to have an amazing team of advance readers and shredders. They give their time and their keen eyes to provide notes, insights, and corrections (dealing wonderfully with my dreaded comma allergy). They help make every book and story go from good to great. Each and every one of them helped make this book fantastic.

THANK YOU

ART SHREDDERS

Amber, Anne Morando, Audrey Cienki

Barbara Hamm, Barbara Henninger, Bennah Phelps, Bethany Showell, Beverly Collie

Cam Skaggs, Carrie Anne O'Leary, Chris Christman II, Colleen Taylor, Connor Jarczynski, Corinne Loder

Darren Musson, Davina 'the Tao of the Comma' Noble, Dawn McQueen Mortimer, Denise King, Diana

Gray, Diane Craig, Diane Kassmann, Dolly Sanchez, Donna Young Hatridge,

Hal Bass, Helen Gibson

Jasmine Davis, Jen Cooper, Joy Kiili, Joy Ollier, Julie Peckett

Karen Hollyhead

Larry Diaz Tushman, Laura Tallman I, Lesley Sharp, Luann Zipp, LZ

Malcolm Robertson, Marcia Campbell, Mary Anne Petruska, Melissa Miller, Melody DeLoach

Nick Church

Pat (the silly sister)

RC Battels, Rene Corrie, Rob Farnham

Sara Mason Branson, Sean Trout, Shannon Owens Bainbridge, Stacey Stein, Stephanie Claypoole, Sue Watts, Susie Johnson

Tami Cowles, Tammy Tushman, Tanya Anderson, Ted Camer, Terri Adkisson, Tommy Owens

Vikki Brannagan

Wanda Corder-Jones, Wendy Schindler

Thanks for Reading

If you enjoyed this book, would you **please leave a review** at the site you purchased it from? It doesn't have to be a book report... just a line or two would be fantastic and it would really help us out!

Made in the USA
Middletown, DE
10 August 2020